Enter Here
An Anthology of Portals
Ed. M. Stevenson and C.J. Subko

Contents

Enter

C.J. SUBKO

YOU HAVE BEEN HERE before.

At least, you remember this place, in the same thin, veiled way you remember your dreams.

It is a forest, dark and deep, and you do not have miles to go before you sleep, for sleep is quite beyond you. Instead, you find yourself wide awake, and wondering.

Where are you?

For this is no ordinary forest. Amidst the trees, needled and tall, are just as many doors. Not doorways, no, but doors, lintel and threshold and casing, each fitted with a panel and a handle or knob. Each of them singular. None of them the same.

Now, you spy a wooden door, teak, perhaps. Now, a gray stone door, glittered with flecks of gold mica.

Which will you choose?

In the end, you do not choose. You close your eyes, and point your feet in a direction, your hand reaching out until your fingertips brush against something cold.

And then, you push.

The Flutist and the Glassblower in the Market of Souls

Claire Jia-Wen

The woman who was once a flutist enters the Night Market still damp from the rains of her world. The place has changed since she was last here, the stalls rearranging themselves, new tents wedging in, others overgrown with shadow and ivy.

But the night still tastes of half-forgotten dreams and something earthier, like sesame; the constellations are in all the same shapes, and we paint a shimmering trail, her boots smudging prints into the soft sugaring of stardust. She pretends nonchalance, stopping here to run her fingers along leaves of the cloud forest and there to speak to the old witch of the marrow. No matter—the catch of her breath and the longing dripping from her gaze reveal the shape of her heart. We know where she wishes to go.

She pulls her hood from her face when she arrives at the stall tucked into the market's half-vanished corner, and the moonlight silvers her skin, which is older than before, new creases like thrice-folded paper.

The glassblower pauses but doesn't set his pipe down. A globule of molten glass glows at its end, like the sun on a roasting skewer. "Tenta," he says, and doesn't give anything more.

"Rook," she replies, and it has been so long since his name has been held in a mouth with so much deliberation, not simply a sound to insist on his attention, but a secret he has shared only with those he loved, once upon a time. "Forge me a blade."

His fingers tighten around the pipe. He doesn't look up at her.

Rook was thirteen when he first met Tenta. He thought she was the prettiest girl he had ever seen, birdlike in a faded nightdress, wrists and throat bare of jewelry: soft skin, delicate bones. Her fingers were curled around a crudely carved flute. She wore cloth slippers that had already worn through against the Market's rough asphalt.

"I wish for you to make me a sword."

"I don't make swords."

She cocked her head to the side. "A knife will do."

"Two stalls down, Old Uncle Goarang makes lockets that can rend a man's soul if he only gives you a smile. And there are a hundred stalls that sell poisons. But my craft does not forge things that will crack the world apart."

Tenta hadn't wanted to crack the world apart. She had only wanted to slip a blade into her father's throat.

Her father wasn't a cruel man, but he was a pragmatic one, and he knew that the House of Mesmer would pay a sum for his talented youngest child, and that it would be a sum great enough to keep his other children's bellies full.

Tenta did not know what would happen after she opened his neck into a tangle of tissues and windpipes. She was only angry.

She had not wept and she had not begged. When her father locked her inside the room she shared with her three sisters so she could not run away before the procurers from the House of Mesmer arrived, she had bowed her head and brought her instrument to her mouth. She blew her lifesbreath into the wood, and when she opened her eyes, a door had opened in her bedroom where there had not been one before. That was how she found the Night Market, and its hundred thousand stars that never move. That was how she found Rook.

Begging wasn't in her nature. She only stood before the glassblower like a specter in frayed cotton, watching the boy's tweezers pull needle-thin limbs from the blowing globule, the glass as viscous as melted candy, so delicate she was sure it would shatter if she startled him. She almost wanted to do it, squeeze his wrist hard enough that he would gasp and release his quarry. Turn the pretty thing into diamond dust.

"It's beautiful," she said.

He held the finished sculpture—a unicorn—out to her.

Offering, she realized.

"If you are talented, you might ask to stay." Rook nodded at the flute. "Visitors can stay in the Market for only one night, vendors until they grow tired of it. You could ply your skills here."

"You don't know I'm good at it," she said, even as her chest swelled with the praise.

"It's obvious."

Tenta knew he was being deliberately vague, fishing for the attention of her questions, but she couldn't resist giving it to him, if only to see the boy's smirk deepen into a smile. "How?"

"You breathe like a flutist," he said. "Like someone who knows what it costs. Not perfect, of course—"

"Thanks—"

"But you could learn here."

For a moment, Tenta hesitated.

The night hung still, holding its breath.

Impossibilities flowered in her mind: staying here and learning from this boy and learning the shape of his breath, the intricately-carved architecture of his throat.

Only for a moment, though.

"I must return." Tenta had sisters and brothers who were always hungry, and speaking to the boy glassblower made her want to be good too.

She'd never had a teacher; she had carved her flute with her own unsteady hands and learned her pitches and melodies from the songbirds. If she could endure the sting of an accidental slip of a scalpel against her palm, she could endure the House of Mesmer. And the House of Mesmer would make sure her siblings were never hungry again.

Yes, that was the thing that must be done.

She swallowed her dread. She had always been such a brave girl. Her hands trembled as she tucked the unicorn into her pocket. "Thank you for your craft, and your kindness," she said to the boy whose face she hoped she would remember enough to touch in her dreams.

"I'm sorry," Rook said, so gently that it could not have only been about the knife.

"I'll make it, but it'll cost you seventy-nine star-teeth," the glassblower says.

Tenta pays with little protest. The girl encased in the swan's nest pavilion demands an unsullied kiss before she lifts her wings for a dance, and the Starved Scryer asks for a memory of decadence before divining the asker's fortunes, but this is good too. Simple.

He takes her coin and turns to the forge. His slender, no-longer-soft fingers pluck a blowpipe and gather molten glass at its end. It does not matter how many times she has seen it, how many times she has dreamed it, the process will never cease to root Tenta with wonder: how Rook rolls the molten glass against the steel table, shaping it like clay, the shapeless thing becoming the symmetrical thing. It could burn her flesh through. She doesn't step back.

He's raising the blowpipe to his lips, about to give the glass its first breath, when Tenta blurts the question that has been scratching at her all this time. "You don't offer a musicians' discount anymore."

His shoulders tighten.

"I forgot I used to do that," he says, which is strange, because it is how Tenta has remembered him for the last twenty years.

Rook hadn't expected to see the little flutist girl ever again. Most of his patrons found the Night Market once and never again: quest-bearing princes who needed a trinket to win a riddling princess's heart, baby dragons just starting to build their hordes of shiny things, a carriongirl who needed to gnaw on something that wouldn't degrade beneath her teeth. It was not hard to convince himself that he preferred this life of transactions, beneath the velvet night and the stars. Everybody who finds him needs him. It's a sweet feeling, being wanted, even if they never stay. He likes to think they remember him.

When the flutist arrived at his stall again, this time in a dark uniform embroidered with the insignia of a snake sinking its fangs into a maiden who smiled as if she enjoyed it, his breath caught.

Tenta said, "Make something for me. Anything."

"Usually, my patrons are more discerning."

She lifted her chin up. "I want to see how you breathe."

Seven words, so insufficient for the fervent curiosity itching beneath her skin; since their first meeting, she had kept herself awake at night imagining the glassblower: how he gathered the world into his lungs, divine for the sliver of a moment, as if destiny were as soft as his glass. When she could take it no longer, the rawness of her imaginings, she played her tune and the door opened in her room in the House of Mesmer.

A smile ghosted across his lips. He still hadn't lifted his gaze to meet hers. "I don't ply my craft without payment."

"I have star-teeth."

"If you play me a song, that will be enough."

"Why?"

"I like to breathe the music in," he said. "Then I can give it to the glass. One of the whistling monks who came through the Night Market, he used to say music was good for the soul. You can feel the glass hum beneath your skin."

Tenta almost said: no, that isn't how it works, music isn't like smoke to be breathed in and out, to be given and taken and given again like a gift. You don't know what you're talking about. Music can't be infused into glass like dye.

But perhaps it can.

Isn't it nice to make beautiful things for once, little musician girl?

She played him her favorite song, the one she had learned from the nightingales in the forest of mists and teeth.

She played him many songs in those months that pulled into years as languidly as glass pulls into handles and legs. She played him the songs she learned from the blackbirds and sparrowhawks, and when she had no more of those to give, she played him the songs that her teachers at the House of Mesmer taught her. In those early years, she was only an apprentice. Things were uncomplicated: a song was a series of notes stitched together into a blanket to wrap around their thin shoulders, that was all.

Though, the House of Mesmer had tattooed their snake and maiden on the back of her shoulder. It had hurt. Tenta pulled down the sleeve of her uniform to show Rook; he ran his fingers over the ink, pretending he didn't wonder how she might shiver if he trailed his touch lower, and Tenta pretending she didn't want him to.

When Tenta had stopped by the witch of the marrow, she had asked the witch for a favor. For old time's sake. The witch had laughed, stirred her tea with her bone-finger, and asked for Tenta's greatest regret.

"It's Rook. You know it's Rook."

The witch laughed her creaking laugh. "But *what about him?* You know I don't like doing a body's last rites without knowing all the things it never should have done."

Tenta shrugged. "Not staying the first time he asked. Mesmering him. I don't know."

She blinked back sudden tears. It all sits beneath her sternum, and she doesn't know what to do with it, that clot of all the words she could have said, all the hurts she could have saved him, saved herself. But mistakes are like glass: they harden, become unworkable, decisions irreversible.

And it has been so many years.

Tenta coughed.

The witch offered Tenta her tea. "For what it's worth," she said, "he still looks up every time he hears flutesong."

We have played host to many from the House of Mesmer. Enchanters and seductresses, schemers and assassins, braided into myriad mythologies: women who sing sailors to their doom, fiddlers who rouse whole villages to dance until their bones poke through the soles of their feet, sing-song girls who infiltrate enemy territory to win wars from the rotted inside. Mesmers have been sold to faerie courts, and high noble houses, and traveling circuses—any institution that might ply the currency of wonder.

Once a mesmer enters into the service of the House, they cannot leave.

Except, of course, to the Night Market. The place burrowed in the gasp between worlds, a haven unbound by laws and gravities. Those refugees of the House reside among us even now: the perfumer who can mix a scent so sweet you'll eat the most rotten of foods with a spritz, the illusionist who can reach into your chest and unhook your heart, the soprano who can sing the dead from their rest, who can sing the comets from the sky.

Strange folk, those ones. But we are happy to accommodate all their startlingly specific requests, if they have something to offer. We have no need for the used-up ones, the ones falling apart too much to perform.

Tenta has drowned the infant sons of rival concubines, and she has played a song so sweet that armies broke their truces in a great river of blood, and yet she still has enough of a heart for it to ache.

"I remember," she says. "I remember I would play you a song and you would make me a sculpture."

Rook lowers the pipe from his lips. "It has been a long time since we cared for that sort of thing." It's been a long time since he's cared for anything.

In time, the flutist and the glassblower learned to love each other.

Kisses stolen behind game booths melted into uniforms tugged open in clumsily barred equipment sheds, limbs entangling in the light of once-used lanterns. They were each other's firsts. It was in these clandestine snatches of time, chests rising and falling in rhythm, laughter and the aftertaste of pleasure sweet on their lips, that he unraveled his past for her.

He had all but been raised in the Night Market, all his memories foregrounded against the eccentric ridge line of stalls and tents. His mother had been from a land of cottages and thorntowers; she had claimed that she could fish the moons from the water and then begged an enchanter to help her prove it to the unwed prince. The only price had been her firstborn, easily promised and easily parted.

The enchanter had been the author of a market between the worlds.

"He brought me here," Rook murmured. "He said I could apprentice in any craft, but I had to work."

"Do you think of your mother often?"

"She didn't love me enough to keep me," Rook said. "She wasn't talented enough to tell the truth of her virtues. I wouldn't have been sustained there, not the way I am here." Here, where everyone is from nowhere, and the bindings of family are as salient as stardust.

Tenta watches the glass cool, the night air kissing it cold and immutable. She imagines plunging it into her own chest.

Rook says she can come look if she wants. The difficult part is over.

They stand so determinedly apart, as if unaccustomed to human touch, which is ironic, because Tenta has parted her legs for beast-kings, and Rook has knelt for poetesses with bloody hands, and each of them was thinking of the other when they did it.

Rook's throat itches but he swallows down the cough. "Do you regret the mesmering?" he murmurs. "Any of it?"

"What difference would it make?"

On the night Tenta mesmered Rook, she had come and asked for a knife.

He said, "You know I won't."

"I do," she said softly, resignedly. "But my teachers asked me to get one from you."

Her teachers had not really needed the knife; the House has hidden rooms lined with blades sharp enough to slice a dragonfly into two symmetrical halves. It was only that the final test of a mesmer is an examination of their emotional agnosticism, their willingness to fulfill the tasks they are assigned. Even if they love their mark.

"Tenta," he said. "Please, don't. Please."

Tenta closed her eyes to play.

It all evens out, doesn't it? He was her first kiss, and she was his first love, and he was the first man she mesmerized, and she was the first woman he forged a weapon for. Completion and ruination. All things equal in the grand calculus of souls.

When Tenta came to the Market tonight, she came to die. She is too old for the House of Mesmer. She is too used for us. She cannot even take a full breath without coughing; she has spent too long breathing the smoke of opium dens, of battlefields laced with gunpowder, and even the grills of the market.

Rook runs a finger along the side of the knife, testing its edge. "Tenta, why did you come here?"

"I wanted a knife."

But they both know she is not a little girl anymore. She does not need a door in her bedroom to obtain a knife. It is no longer her enemies she is trying to kill, in any case.

"You wanted something, yes," he murmurs. "It isn't a knife."

"I wanted to die. I have my rites sorted out with the witch of the marrow."

"There are easier places to die than here."

He's making her say it. Petty, petty boy.

She takes a half breath, pushes the words from her throat. "I came because I wanted to see you one last time, and I didn't want to die without having told you I'm sorry. I have been sorry from the moment I played that first note, and I know it doesn't matter because I did it anyway. I have spent my life justifying every subsequent wicked act with this fact: if I could do it to the boy I loved, I can do it to anyone, I have already ruined myself and none of it matters at all. That's it." She juts her chin up, the motion so familiar Rook almost chokes on the emotions tangling in his own throat.

"Does that make any difference?"

Finally, he lifts his gaze to meet hers, and she rediscovers the impossible blue of his eyes. She remembers that she once imagined sinking into that blue as she held him and whispered all the things she was scared of, all the futures she didn't know she could survive.

"Yes," he says hoarsely.

We have played host to a hundred thousand stories, you must understand. If we interfered even once, that would be very unfair to all the times we did not. We watch tragedies unfurl, and we let them.

"Now give me the knife," Tenta says.

Once, the Archer King drew his yew-wood bow and shot down eleven suns. A sorcerer with silver bands encircling his wrists folded ten thousand paper cranes to flutter up to the moon and collect bits of its flesh, to be stitched into a veil for his prince's bride. In three hundred and five years, a weaver girl will unravel a patch of the sky and make a noodle soup of the threads to save her ailing mother.

Sun, moon, sky—those lesser heavenly bodies can be stolen, reappropriated, transmuted. But the Archer King, the sorcerer, the weaver girl, they knew, know, will know: the stars cannot be dislodged from their perches. They are not fool enough to try.

The glassblower who has always kept his eyes down finally lifts his gaze to the sky; the man who has never asked for his own freedom asks the stars he has never believed in for the most impossible thing in the world. He is not stupid. He has lived his whole life among these mercurial stalls. He knows we have had so many chances to intervene in so many tragedies, and we have not. He asks anyway.

He says: you brought me here when I was a boy and I never complained, I worked your forges and delighted your patrons, and I have never prayed and never asked and never cursed you, but I am asking now, I am asking even though I know I will not be beautiful and useful to you much longer, I am asking you to save the woman I love, and I can't give you any reasons besides that I love her. Please.

"The trick to breathing," Rook said, a long time ago, "is to use your whole body for it, not only your lungs. You are capable of holding more air than you think. All the winds of the world can be sieved in and out of the human body if you can control it."

With a healthy dollop of skepticism, Tenta tried to act out what the glassblower was describing. The air tickled her throat in the wrong way, and she coughed.

"It's not a natural process," Rook said quickly, rushing to mend his credibility before the failure sank in. "I learned the technique from a passing-through monk. I can teach it to you too."

Tenta tasted a lingering ashiness in her mouth, the leftover smoke from the grills that offer flying squid skewers and the dragon-kettles hissing with steam a few stalls away. "It damages you, doesn't it? Taking all the smoke in too."

"Yes," he said. "I don't mind."

She nodded. "Then I won't either."

Tenta did not know that tomorrow, her teachers at the House would ask for the ultimate test of her loyalty, and Rook did not know that in seven years, he would forge a weapon for a boy who sought to kill his father, but all the fortune tellers and forgone destinies would not have mattered in that moment stolen from the jaws of time; it would not have made the flutist shift her head from his shoulder, nor would it have shriveled the blooming tenderness in the glassblower's chest when he gazed down at the girl nestled against him. It was hard to believe that she had not been shaped to fit perfectly against him, that his history had not been carved so that she would be less alone in the dizzying spiderweb of souls that makes up our lives. Twin lungs, sieving the dust and music and pollutions of the world, in tandem, in parallel.

Rook brushed a tendril of hair from Tenta's face, though it had not been falling into her eyes. "Sometimes," he said, "I imagine that the stars can be scattered as easily as dandelion fluff, with a single exhale."

The Seam Ripper Above God's Navel

SARA S. MESSENGER

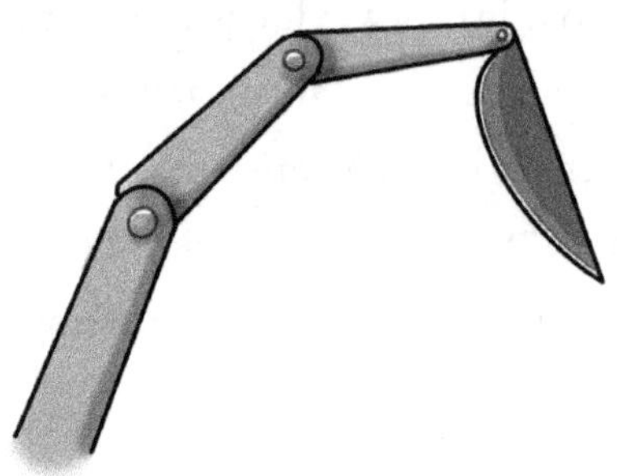

ENDEL, YOU ARE ONLY five. You like to curl around your iPad, you like to watch videos from Animal Planet and horror video games and indie animations and maggot farms. You like to go outside, into the solarponic garden, when I let you; you like to take baths in cornstarch and water. You flail to the chirp of birds. I've made you special spoons to help your grip; I've installed ramps and swabbed the floor thrice daily; I've taught you how to read and speak, and you've picked up on both faster than I'd hoped. But in due time you will not have any of this. You will have no iPad, no YouTube or books, no porcelain bathtub with the accessible ramp. You will not have verbal language. Eventually, you will forget how to read altogether. You will not *need* any of this. And all of this means you may never really comprehend this letter, this complicated letter so full of vocabulary you have yet to learn—so this is a selfish letter. Instead of writing this I should be holding you. Please forgive your Baba. I only ever tried my best.

I had a hysterectomy when I was getting my doctorate degree. A hysterectomy is when they take out the part of Baba that would have made Wendel. And they did the hysterectomy but not properly, with the chronic pain that ensued, and so I had no reason to trust surgeons nor standard medicine. I took matters into my own hands. And so you arrived on the cot in the corner of my laboratory, under the great angular shadow of the Seam Ripper. When I lifted you from the sheets I was afraid of your fragility. You were almost semiliquid, as if I could have broken your skin if I pressed my finger with intent. I couldn't look at your face yet. I just cut your precious umbilical cord, swaddled you, and wandered around the operating table, running my free hand over my gears and grommets and circuit diagrams and toolboxes.

I couldn't figure out how to get you to latch on to the bottle, and I couldn't figure out your mouth, and I never did well with anything reminding me of my chest, even after top surgery. I ended up feeding you formula soaked in cloth. I'm sorry about that too. Your cries made me cry. They were beautiful, like alien birds drowning in a kaleidoscopic lagoon. I'm sorry for the big words. After you calmed, I laid you in a cradle I'd bought off a seedy online shop. Lest you forget: the world was normal when you were born. The electrical grids were still running and the Internet was still intact and chasms were not splitting the earth and burping ash into the sky.

One day, after you grow up, you may become consumed by anger and despair, like so many have, but if you are lucky, there will be nothing to be angry about. Not where you are. This is my hope. You will learn eventually about gods, which is not my *hope*—it is inevitable. You will learn about how they fight in the metaphysical plane and eat each other, how they depend on each other like dominoes in their ecosystem, how they take many faces and enter dreams to beckon believers. How, where you and I live, the people who used violence to populate the land brought a tall, single God with them, a Christian God. How my parents introduced me to Him. I saw Him in my dreams, flickering in and out of the dark in the corner of my eye. How when I told my girlfriend, she did not understand. If those who rule your society use their God to justify making your transition illegal—if your parents use their God to justify their hatred of you and who you become—you may find Him hiding in the dark corner yourself. And as you turn away, you will feel His hot breath on your back as He begins to salivate. You might find yourself taking one step, then another, away from Him, down the road of a hateful agnosticism, confused, guttering steeples behind your eyelids.

But your feet hurt. And you have two hands and an ache to do something, anything.

To do the impossible.

As I write this now, you're in the other room as red emergency broadcasts scroll across your iPad—among the multitude of other apocalyptic concerns, the United Astronomy Center is blaring about a dark mass in our atmosphere. Uncommunicative. Fast descending.

And as you ache, you might find yourself burning to ask: Baba, how do I stop Him? How do I end this heat constricting my chest and silencing my voice and threatening to stop my heart?

I'll give you my answer here: Killing God is not the hard part. The hard part is luring Him in. The hard part is stealing close enough, in your dreams, to stab.

You have never liked the Seam Ripper, Wendel—much like the only other person you have ever met, my old girlfriend, Moira. I admit while I find it beautiful, there's a certain austerity in its design—the stout, sterile fuel chamber, the hulking pipes, the spindly mechanical limb that arcs twenty feet high above the platform, ending in an iridescent, oily blade. Cutting-edge innovation is no beauty pageant, as I used to tell Moira, gentle pageant queen she was. I began building the Seam Ripper a decade before you arrived, but my use of it on the day you were born made it clear extensive modifications had to be made if I ever hoped to turn it on again. Simply, in the five years since then, you've grown up alongside it. You both have grown together. But though you've been ambivalent to its gleaming architecture since you were an infant, I've noticed you've become afraid of it now—since I gave you an iPad, you have begun prodding at my misanthropy.

You have just inched into the room. A shred of silky web is stuck to your cheek. You say, politely, as you always do: *Baba, why can't I go to the 'ponics garden? Can I go outside instead?*

But I am busy, busy monitoring metrics and writing this letter. The Seam Ripper thrums behind me, and you must see the sweat soaking through my clothes, the painful tensing of my shoulders, because at my glance you turn tail and disappear beyond the doorway again.

Behind the curtain, on the operating table, is God's navel. It's a huge, severed thing with fibrous strands erupting from the bloodied end of it. It's roughly the height of a five-year-old: it's roughly the height of you. God—would you have guessed?—had an outie. I've sketched it in a research notebook—I have a great many—but I will only pack one for you: my exploration log from my only foray into a Seam.

If you find it within yourself to read it, you will be more prepared for what's to come. I've calibrated the Seam Ripper to excruciating precision, so it will open the same one again, within a negligible margin of error—let me use large words, as I have already been. Let me write with my hand one last time, to someone in my life. In an hour, I will explain all this to you verbally in gentler terms, using words like *portal, another world, maggot-friends.* But here I will indulge in technicality.

Dimensions are like onion skins, Wendel, and they are layered on top of one another, oscillating at different frequencies, so close that in my dreams I taste them. And yet, we worlds are worlds apart.

I've built a machine that tears a hole in the onion's skin. This *fixation* of mine is what had me shunned in undergraduate, exiled from my doctoral degree, scraping at menial labor until my mother, thankfully, died. But you know the world like I know the world: how we both have never fit in. How I could never enroll you in school or take you beyond the backyard meadow, how you ask questions and cry out of the loneliness. How when you were three, you escaped from your nursery and ran into Moira. The only other person you've ever met. You gazed up at her.

Her face curled in revulsion. *God.*

I carried you away, and then I told her the truth about the Seam Ripper, and then we fought, we argued for months, and she asked to see you again, and then I buried her outside in the back of our solarponic garden. I could not spare—that you might see her revulsion again.

I hope you feel I have given you all the love I could offer. And I hope that I have.

Moira never felt that I had, but how could I, when I've seen what's beyond the Seam. *Who's* beyond the Seam. How silken and humid their forests are, how slick their colorful swampy floors, how tenderly they care for one another. How tenderly they cared for me.

To slice the navel into thin sections, I use my overhead saw—the thinner, to burn quicker, the better. All those years ago, I suspended your umbilical cord in a shatterproof jar, and that I've packed in your backpack. I hope they enjoy the gift. I could not think of anything more fitting.

It was they who introduced me to their transcendental philosophy. The first time I got the Seam Ripper to work I became injured, thoroughly, by passing through—spinal compression and constriction that left me with pain and constant vertigo. When I arrived, I steadied myself against the arcing arm, stumbled off the platform, and lasted only three days in the dusky plainsland before collapse.

There, they found me and let me ride upon their backs, away from the Seam Ripper and the unforgiving plains. They allowed me deep into their swamps. I witnessed, borne by their warmth, their sumptuous fanged fruits, the nutrient-rich soil, the shrieking birds, muscular and razor-sharp. They, with their simple, supple, ringed bodies, so akin to a fly's larvae, buried me in the peat at my assent. I dreamt things, beautiful things, full of gelatinous landscapes, and colorful birds who circled overhead, eager to speak to me. And after months, when I resurfaced, my compatriots acted upon me with silks, nested with me, massaged my limbs and fed me brood jelly.

I was not healed, not entirely, since even there the body holds its old wounds, but I was much improved, and would have been much worse without their care. They divulged to me, in their language based solely on taps and touch, that my injuries were consistent with what some of them called *travel shock.*

When they pass through their distance-collapsing lagoons, if there is a lack of vegetation powering the area, they experience full-body elongation and compression, pain for months afterward. Their bodies are more malleable than mine, of course—not even bones—so travel-shock presented more acutely in my system.

They welcomed me. We feasted on birds together, explored and teased together, and at night, we laid close in intricate nests. Plainly, they told me: Whatever lagoon you used to come here was not powered enough. You have suffered for it. Should you attempt to cross that lagoon again, unprepared, you know it will be your last.

I said, despairing: So there is not enough power here for my machine.

They did not understand *machine*, so I translated it as *blade*. They said, There is a power greater than vegetation. Then they gestured up, at the strange, hulking birds.

They said, those are gods, little gods that wander about the forest. They eat and beget each other. Find the strongest little god you can. Then find the one who birthed it. Or find a god who has birthed. Either. You know what to do from there.

The day I finally came back to Earth, I removed the god-parent's dead, feathered body from the Seam Ripper's fuel chamber. Only then did I realize how swollen its stomach had become. And so, still dizzy from how vast the sky looked in the plainsland, I laid its body down, on my cot, and I reached for my scalpel, and gently, so gently, out you came.

Upon my return, I began the five-year modification process. And now, I hope—after all—that the Seam Ripper is reliable. The fuel source is not. I dreamed and dreamed, but I could not find the one who birthed God,

Wendel. It seems they fled this dimension, ashamed, or never stepped foot here in the first place.

There are other gods I could have hunted, but He was so attracted to me, to my pulling away, to the guttering steeples behind my eyes, to the prospect that He could lose His territory, my mind, His birthright. I was patient and cunning and true. I meant every step I took away from Him, though each one took a toll on my soul. And when He brought Himself, fuller than life, to me—when He, from His seat on high, lique-fied Himself in entirety and poured into my unconscious psyche—when He opened His mouth to swallow me in the dead of night, Wendel—I was ready.

I couldn't bury God's corpse in the garden. I left Him in the sky.

That is why you cannot go outside.

I washed the slices of navel in crude oil. As I did, I found myself reflecting on Moira. I thought she'd—maybe she'd make a good mother for you. If she could accept me, my bouts of chronic pain, my black-market hormones and parental hatred and social difficulties, then maybe she could have accepted you. Maybe she was on the road—to accepting you. But we fought about the strangest parts of me: about the Seam Ripper, about the existence of beings who treated me kindly, about you. And now, we will never know.

After much reflection, I don't think it was the *idea* of the Seam Ripper that repulsed my colleagues and my lover—it was my enormous hatred of this world, and my single-minded drive, and the sheer lengths I would go to get it working.

They were right, in the end. That I had to fell a god—a keystone species that has cannibalized and siphoned so many others, one who allowed the world to hate me so, who let my parents, my colleagues, my girlfriend, my *society* be so incompatible with me—felt like just an upside.

I'm sorry I'm being spiteful about myself, Wendel. I hope when you read this, once you're older, you will understand. Or maybe you will not. You will be among better people. Your people. You do not know it yet, but I have been teaching you their language when I tuck you in bed: a tap on the temple means *I love you.*

I've opened the Ripper's fuel incinerator. I've placed the cuts of navel inside. I've run the calculations: the vestige of God's parent, Their umbilical connection, is not enough to power a Seam crossing for two.

I want to say it tears me apart to send you alone, and I expected it to. But I've done so much in this life. I'm so tired.

I brought you into this world, and I *will* send you to a place where you are loved.

I will not do to you what God did to me.

Tap. Do you remember what this means?

And my last truth: I don't think I'm good to you. I haven't been good to anyone else.

I'm about to seal this letter and call you into the room, watch you squirm across the tile for the last time. I'll attach your backpack to your harness, kiss your soft, moist cheek, wipe errant strands of silk from your tail. I'll tell you to open this letter when you're older and braver and strong enough to hate me more.

As the ceiling trembles above us, I will tell you that I've destroyed this wretched world for your passage. I will not tell you I am selfish. I could say I hope for forgiveness, but what would forgiveness do for me?

Instead, I hope you will be okay.

I've called your name. I'm licking the edge of the envelope.

Good Girls of the Salt

B.L. JASPER

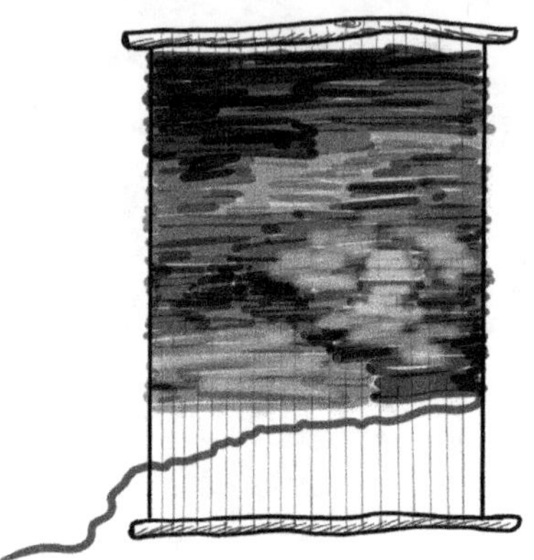

MY CHILDREN GNAW ON the trees and I let them. Staring out the window from my loom, I don't protest as they snap off twigs, crusted with sweet sap, and chew. It is bad for their stomachs, their teeth, their throats—but what can I do? The mewling of their bellies will drive me to madness.

Coralie, the eldest, teaches the others to look for sugars crystallized on the joints of maple branches. She does this because the salt of my milk has dried, breast tissue dwindling to nothing as the winter starves us out.

My fingers return to their work. I will either finish this tapestry or we will die.

Consuming an entire wall of our log cabin, a scene has been woven. It has taken many years, and the sheep who once provided the threads for my loom are long dead, the wool only a memory beneath my fingertips.

Still, I will not be discouraged. Our fate rests on my embroidery needle, and the deftness of ravenous hands.

"Mimän!" Perla, my middle daughter, rushes in, her hands full of something dark and ropy. The way she calls me mother sounds murky out of water, and yet it never fails to bring a smile to my face. "Look what I've found." She holds her hands out to me, revealing long stringy roots, dirt still clinging to them. They have a reddish hue, and as I pluck them from her cold fingers she bounces with excitement.

"They would be perfect right here, don't you think?" She points to the tapestry, where waves lap at a rock and the setting sun casts no reflection on the water. Her sea-dark eyes turn to me, hopeful.

"Just so, my pearl." I set aside the needle I am working with and pick up another, crudely made from the very same maple tree my daughters now devour. Dusting off the lingering soil, I thread the root through the needle and begin to stitch bullion knots into the water around the rock. Perla watches with rapt attention as the sunset comes to life through her contribution.

She has never been to this place, the beach where I once sunbathed with my own sisters on coal-black sand, and yet she has known it all her life, its image hanging on this wall, growing more fond with each passing day. When we are free of Outis and we walk the sands of our home once again, she will know it in her heart. The ocean will call to her.

I hope.

We both stand back and observe the tapestry. It is so close to being finished, but something is still missing—something opalescent, something blue. I tilt my head to study it from another angle, but the gap in my memory eludes me.

"Mimän!" Coralie interrupts our observation. She tracks snow past the threshold and I cast a chastising look her way.

"Coralie." Her name is my song, bubbling like tide foam from salt-hungry lungs. It is hard to discipline my girls, harder still when I see myself in them. "The snow," I say, gesturing with distaste at the floor. "You know better."

"But Mimän, someone is coming." She points to the small trail coming from the woods, and her expression is telling.

"Your father?"

We share a look. "No, thank the tides." Coralie mimics a phrase I use often. "Taller. Bigger. Blond hair."

"Must be Hal, then. If we play our cards right, my girls, we will eat meat tonight. You know what to do." I nod toward the window, where Nyria, the youngest, still gnaws on the twigs her siblings have discarded. "Gather yourselves and become scarce."

Once, I'd turned away the men who came to see me. These men had heard tell of a sea-woman kept in the woods, and they came to gawk. Was I beautiful? Hideous? Were my teeth sharp, and were there webs between my fingers? Did my tail remain? Was I biddable, beddable?

That was before Outis, miserable father of my children, left us here to starve for months at a time, stranded a world away from the crashing waves and coral spirals of our home. A home I have not seen in twelve years, but whose sea foam lullabies nevertheless hum in my bones. The crosshatched, silvery scars of his ropes, which pulled me up out of the water like the day's catch, still glisten on my back under moonlight. What devilry, to weave ropes with iron.

The scent of my burning flesh and scales wafts, potent, through my memory.

"Mimän!" Perla tugs my roughspun dress, snapping me back to the moment. "Can I stay?"

My eyes blink, transparent membranes dipping and receding as I separate the memory of my capture from this moment. My gaze slips from the distant path to my daughter, and I reach to stroke her silk-soft hair. What will her fins look like, when we return to the sea? Will they be feathered at the ends, like mine, or sleek, like her aunt's? Will her scales be moonglow white, like her grandmother's, or as golden as lost treasure? How sharp will her teeth be? How long her claws?

I hope she has a voice that will lure men to their deaths by the hundreds.

I smile at her. "No, my pearl, not this time."

Her dainty feet drag as she mopes from the house, and I could cry at the thinness of her from behind, the nubs of her spine stark where her collar dips. Back home the changing of the seasons did not concern me. We hunted and we foraged and we were never hungry. But Outis dug iron into the earth here, a perimeter to keep me contained, and I cannot leave to seek out food. Would that I could lure animals into my domain, but all I seem to be able to catch is men.

"Ho!" Hal's resonating voice calls out from the tree line. "Anyone home?"

With determination, I become as the iron that holds me here: unflinchingly strong. My children need me and I will provide, no matter the cost.

We eat roasted venison, potatoes, and onions. It is vile, but sustaining. My daughters do not have the same qualms as me when it comes to consuming land-creatures, and I hope they do not mind overmuch when we're returned to the sea. I miss the fine taste of mollusk and the fresh crunch of spine in yearling fish. I comfort myself that it cannot be any worse than eating maple twigs. They will adapt.

As we eat, I study the tapestry. The girls chatter, the sound of it washing over me like the gentle lap of waves. I close my eyes and something glitters in the water, sparkling against the black sand like a fallen star. I drag myself to it, claws sinking into the beach; the feel, even in my imagination, is satisfyingly tactile. The sun glows orange in the distance, just as it does on my tapestry, this single moment caught in wool and memory.

The object of my attention sparkles again as the waves lap against my soft dorsal fin. It flutters, featherlike in the push and pull of the water. I submerge my head to get a closer look at the shiny item, and discover a broken mollusk shell. The nacre is blue, and as I reach for it, ready to carry it home and tie it in my hair, it eludes me, and is swept into the sea.

My eyes snap open, focusing on the tapestry. And I see it then, the missing piece, and I know how to get us home.

Another suitor appears two days later, and finishing the tapestry is so close I can taste it like fresh oysters on my tongue. Clynt demands noth-ing of me, unlike the other suitors. His smile is easy, his manner kind, his shoulders broad. I hate him less than I hate everyone else. If he was on a ship, staring at me over the railing, I would not sing him to his death.

He trudges through the snow ahead of me, and we are very close to the place where I cannot pass—the iron line. Still, I've been thinking about this problem, and a bit of trickery may be all I need.

"Are you sure there's a pond up here?" Clynt asks, taking my hand to help me step over a fallen log. His boots are more stable than my slippers, a fact I will use to my advantage.

"Yes, Outis used to take me there." Before I'd tried to run away. Before he'd created the iron line. Before my girls. So long ago now.

"You don't have to stay with him, you know. I have a very comfortable cabin down in the valley. The girls can come." Clynt looks at me over his shoulder, and there is a spark of hope in his eyes, though we've had this conversation before. Better the devil I know, and I know Outis. How ruthless he is and what he will do to keep me. We would not be safe with Clynt.

"If he's not back by spring, I promise to consider it." It's a lie—we will be gone long before then. Tonight even, if I can find what I need at the pond. Still, it won't do to crush Clynt's hope, so I smile at him.

My fangs are long gone, shriveled and receded into my gums. I have not been able to use them to crack mollusks and hunt fish, and like so much of me now, they appear human. Twelve years without the sea will do that to a mermaid.

It is for the salt that I do what comes next.

We come upon a patch of ice, and I place my foot in just the wrong spot. My legs go from under me, and I crash into the snow, my ankle throbbing with no small amount of pain.

Clynt turns and rushes back to my side. "Are you all right?"

"Yes," I pant as he helps me sit up. His warm hand is anchored at my back as he assists me in sitting. "It's just my ankle…" I wince, prodding at the joint.

"Let me take a look." Clynt's fingers gingerly touch my ankle and when I do not cry out, he rolls the ankle to test for breaks. Finding none, he looks up at me, relief clear in his expression. "Not broken. Can you stand?"

"Will you help me?"

"Of course."

With effort, I am on my feet again and the pain is not so bad, but I look at the upwards trail with trepidation.

"Perhaps we should turn back," Clynt suggests.

"The girls are looking forward to fish. I cannot disappoint them. Will you carry me? It's not much further, and if I rest there, I'll be able to endure the return trip."

He looks at me with such uncertainty I think I may have ruined my chances of getting to the pond, but when I add a soft "please," he buckles. I do not have eyes as dark as the midnight sea for nothing.

Clynt's arms and shoulders are strong, and I am starving. He carries me with ease.

The ploy works. As he steps over the iron line, I feel no sharp sting. The skin of my feet does not begin to smoke. My heart does not squeeze and palpate. And then we are beyond it. He carries me up a curved deer path, over a small crest, and there it is: Calico Lake.

The lake is named for its speckled shores, a mixture of dark basalt and brown septarian, chunks of light limestone and peppery granite. But interspersed among the rocks is the very thing I came for, in a greater number than I could have hoped: clamshells.

The lake clams have left me an abundant collection to look through, and I know in my salt-laden bones that only one of them will be perfect. I must find it.

Clynt sets me down on the shoreline, and with a pick tucked into his belt, chips away at the ice until the dark depths of the lake are revealed. We toss out the fishing lines, anchoring them to shore with spikes driven into the sandy ground. That done, I limp along the shoreline collecting shells. I gather them in my skirts, dusting snow away to find any that might be trying to hide. When Clynt sees what I am doing, he begins to collect the shells also. We do not talk, and that is another reason I do not hate Clynt like I hate the others.

When our fishing lines are full and my skirts are laden with shells, I lay them out on the beach next to the fire Clynt has built for us, and study each shell intently. The sheen inside must be perfect, with a blue undertone. Many are too white and pearlescent to suit my purpose, and many too dark, but at last I settle on one that feels just right.

I tuck it with great care into my pocket, and together we venture down the path toward home. When we arrive at the iron line, I plead exhaustion, and Clynt carries me. In warm arms, I am placed back in my prison. But it will not be for much longer now.

I first realize something is wrong when I see the smoke coming from the chimney of our house. It is robust and smells of meat. There was no meat left when Clynt and I banked the fire and set off this morning.

I begin to run, limping as quickly as I can, and as I do I see the other signs. A sled in the yard, still unpacked and laden with supplies. A set of fresh footprints in the snow.

Outis.

I stumble as I enter the clearing where our cottage sits, and my knees skid on ice. Damn the clumsiness of human anatomy.

Clynt is somewhere behind me, probably deciding whether to stay or vanish into the woods before he can be caught. What he does is of no concern to me; only worry for my daughters fills my head.

I crash in through the side door, panting. Outis is too smart for me to toy with him, but I try anyway. "Outis? You're home!"

The scene before me stops me in my tracks. Perla sits on our wooden dining bench in front of the fire, and behind her, Outis braids her hair in intricate fisherman-like webbing. The same webbing he used to snare me, and if that is not a message, I am not a mermaid. But Perla is blissfully unaware of the warning in his actions, and her eyes are closed, a look of contentment on her face.

Nyria, the baby, plays by the fire with a wooden ship on wheels and a carved mermaid toy. Only smart Coralie looks afraid. She stands beside the fire with a long wooden spoon, stirring aromatics in the cauldron while meat roasts on the spit. Her eyes dart between us, as though she knows the situation could degrade with the slightest movement.

Nyria and Perla hardly remember their father, but Coralie has seen what I could not hide: the bruises, the silver scars, the jump in my movement as Outis's voice snaps like canvas in an angry wind. She knows what the suitors seek when they arrive, and she knows I am not allowed to leave this clearing.

"My love," Outis says, his fingers working the last of Perla's braids. "Where have you been?"

The question is a knife unsheathed.

"Only foraging," I say, careful not to lie.

"For what? I see nothing. Where is your basket?" His eyes narrow on my damp hems and sodden slippers, and the sand and dirt smudging the front of my homespun dress.

"Food," I reply in as vague terms as possible, and it is true. The fish on our line would attest to that. "You have been gone so long. The girls have been very hungry."

I take a step into the cabin and open my arms to Perla, trying to get her to leave her father's reach. "Your hair looks lovely, Perla. Did you thank your father?"

Outis's eyes meet mine, and they are the dark of a storm. "With whom?"

Perla turns to her father and hugs him around his waist. He wraps an arm around her, holding her there, and repeats his question.

"With whom?"

"I'm sure I don't know what you mean," I placate, taking a step toward Perla.

His hand tightens on her shoulder as he smiles. "The tracks in the yard beg to differ. Unless your feet have suddenly become the size of a man's?" He looks pointedly at my sodden slippers.

"My pearl, why don't you go out into the yard and gather some more wood for the fire?" I suggest, attempting to shoo her out the door and away from her father.

Blessedly, he lets her go.

The silence is thick in the air, and a sudden backdraft of smoke from the fireplace leaves the cloying smell of roasting meat and onions over everything.

"We've been very hungry," I say.

"Yes, little Perla told me all about it while I did her hair," Outis says, taking a step toward me. "She's told me of the lean times, but you're always saved, aren't you? Men, delivering meat, eggs, fish, vegetables..." Another step. "So many deliveries."

By the fireplace, Coralie clutches the spoon to her chest, fear imprinted on her face, in the tightness of her lips, the watery look of her eyes.

"What did you expect me to do, *husband?*" I spit the word like the venom it is.

"Wait, like I commanded you to, *wife.*" His presence is overpowering. It always has been. Never was there kindness, and barely civility.

"We were starving, Outis." I find the iron in me and use it against him. "You left us to *die.*"

"Better that you did." He moves to strike, as quick as the lunge of a marlin after its prey.

The moment unspools around me.

Coralie's spoon slams down on Outis's wrist so hard the handle cracks, and the spoon end goes flying, clattering against the floor in a corner. Outis cries out, pulling his hand back, and he turns toward Coralie, his face beet red with fury. She holds what's left of the spoon in front of her, a sharp vengeance to her I've never seen before.

Tides—my daughter, my beautiful daughter, so full of the fury of the sea. It will accept her, I know it will. The ocean is our home, our mother, and she wants us back.

I leap on Outis's back as he moves toward Coralie. His balance is thrown off, but he does not stumble. My arms constrict around his throat, my legs around his middle.

"Coralie! My pocket! Get the shell." I grunt with exertion, but I am no match for Outis. He is well fed and made of muscle. But, starved as I am, I will not go down without a fight.

I miss my claws, those sharp and precise tools of my youth, but they were the first thing to go.

Coralie darts in and rifles around in my pocket until she finds the shell, taking it straight to the tapestry. Though I have never explicitly told her what I am trying to do, she knows. The sea sings to her the same way it does to me. When she closes her eyes, she hears the rush of the waves, the cries of the gulls.

"Crush it and finish the tapestry. Weave them in, let the image—" I grunt as Outis grabs my braid and yanks "—call to you."

Outis's strong arms reach over his back to yank me away. I panic and let go. He turns, as quick as the lash, and a fist crashes into my cheek. I am thrown back, hitting the bench with a thud. Blinking the stars from my eyes, I realize Perla is on the threshold, and behind her, Clynt.

Clynt takes one look at me on the floor, another at Outis, red-faced and huffing, and he steps into the room. I am grateful for his intervention, and do not waste a moment of it.

I rush to Coralie and take the shell fragments from her bleeding hands. They have cut her, but the ocean will love her blood, just as it loves mine. "Go," I urge. "Gather Perla and Nyria, come back to me, we must go *now.*"

"But Mimän—"

I cut her off. "Now is not the time to argue. We leave now, or we will not leave at all."

Behind me Clynt and Outis wrestle, dangerously close to the fireplace one moment, knocking cups and trenchers from the wall the next. Dried lavender rains down upon them.

I pick at the fragments of shell in my palm, looking for the perfect ones, and weave them into the tapestry. Piece after piece, I recreate my memory exactly.

I know the moment the image is complete.

The feeling of comfort moves through me like the swell of a wave, and it pulls me out to sea with a great tug. I smell salt air, wet stones, moss, tidal swill. I know the darkness of the black sand, feel its heat on my back, long to breathe in the water.

"Mimän! He's going to kill papa!" Perla is crying now, and my eyes snap open. I cannot waste time in memory. We have to move.

"Hold her," I say, shoving Perla into Coralie, who holds Nyria. My daughters huddle together as I rush to the fireplace and grab a piece of wood from among the flames. My skin is seared, but it is nothing. Soon I will be of the sea, and the sea will be of me.

I back toward the tapestry and see that the odds of the fight have flipped. Clynt struggles against Outis now, and something in my heart hesitates to leave him here to die.

"Clynt," I call out. "What can I do?"

"Nothing," he replies, his hands shooting up to grasp Outis around the neck. "Whatever you are planning, do it!"

My hatred for Outis swirls black with all the potency of a hurricane, and I grab the stool where I've spent hours working my loom. The wood is so familiar, almost beloved. I fling it, one handed and with all my might, relishing the snap against Outis's spine.

With that, the world of men is no longer my concern.

"Grab on to my skirts." My children do as they are told, good girls of the salt that they are, and we step toward the ocean.

The tapestry opens for us. It carries us through on an inhale, and the lungs of the ocean exhale us onto shore. I take one last look at the cabin in the woods, so far away from the sea it almost starved the life from me, and I spit on the floor. My spit smokes like acid, and I light the tapestry on fire behind us.

Twelve years to the day and I am home. The girls cling to my skirts, but I need not have worried. Already the salt changes us. Their hair sparkles like silk charmeuse, their eyes glint like fish scales. Their fingernails change to the nacre of black pearl, elongating. Their gills begin to flutter.

When Coralie smiles at me, her teeth are as sharp as daggers.

The sea calls to us, mother that she is, and like obedient daughters, we run to her.

Into her arms we dive.

Saltwater floods our lungs, but my daughters were brought up on salt milk and song, and there is no cause to fear. We are home.

Somewhere in the Nowhere

MICHAEL BETTENDORF

THE BEING SPEAKS TO me at night during the cold melancholic hours where time bends around itself, when anything sounds plausible. It speaks to me in contorted groans. Hunger pangs. Grotesque noises that my own stomach mimics in pathetic biological emulation. A tiny squish of stomach acid and bile that I throw up and swish in my mouth just to remember how humanity tastes.

The first thing I need you to understand is that I do not understand anything. Everything you are going to find written along the walls of this godforsaken lighthouse is the truth as I know it—or rather, the truth as I have perceived it. I am of sound mind and body. I want you to believe me. I need you to. Beyond that, I don't know what to tell you. Make of it what you will.

The second thing I need you to understand is that I am trying to help.

The lighthouse beacon is lit, not as a warning, but a guide. It's always been lit. It will always be lit, to bring the Being near to feed.

Unless I can stop it.

I'm trying.

I'm sorry.

I'll try harder.

You'll see my name, Curtis, scrawled in a few places. It may seem insignificant—childish—like I'm claiming ownership of this lighthouse simply by writing my name here and there, but I can assure you it made sense to me when I first began. An act of measuring distance. An act of reminding myself who I am.

As I climb, I stop to peer out the lighthouse windows when my head can handle it. The glass panes are bubble domes that appear both concave and convex. Don't misunderstand me. They are not flat panes of glass. They are not planar. The windows are a geometrical contradiction that my eyes cannot parse together. The glass strains my eyes to the point of leaky double vision. I wipe my eyes, concentrate, and press my cheek to the cold surface to inspect it. I cup my hands around one eye, hoping my altered depth-perception will reveal something to me. I pull back to recenter. My skin leaves an oily smudge on the pane; a foggy blur remains from my breath. I tap the glass, soft at first, trying to determine its thickness. I tap again.

Tap. Tap. Tap.

I listen for echoes.

I tap harder, until my fingernails crack and chip—fragile eggshells, like those I see broken in nests of sinew outside among the spired branches. Have you ever seen a newborn bird? Slimy and bald and so, so small inside their broken shells, carrying the DNA of the oldest creatures on this planet. This planet that is incredibly young and insignificant.

Have you seen a newborn bird fly in clumsy and reckless descent? I have.

I don't believe the creatures outside are newborn birds, but they resemble them, with sparse tufts of bioluminescent feathers and flesh so pale you can see road maps of blood vessels underneath. They fly by the windows on occasion and perch on rocky spires like bats while they feed their young. Eyes red. Embers of torment.

I pick at the inkwell on my wrist and write on the stone walls along the spiral stairs. You'll find a lot of information along the walls. I hope it's useful. I hope I'm useful.

Let me tell you what I remember before I crossed the threshold of the lighthouse into this nowhere-place.

I was happy. Ambitious. Lost. I wore out dozens of library cards. Attended every free academic talk I could. Walked miles upon miles through public museums and exhibits. I didn't go to school. I tried. Dropped out more than once. I had no money. No home, either. That was fine; I preferred to sleep with the stars.

Perhaps the Being is a star.

I don't really believe that. So many of the stars we can see are already dead, their light a silent death rattle. A reminder of how small we are, and of their lasting grandeur.

The Being is very much alive.

Moisture seeps through a crack in the window and trickles down the wall to where I rest. It isn't water, but it's all that's available, so I drink. It is sweet like nectar, which might explain the curious hummingbirds I've seen flutter by—decaying glints of flimsy bone and beak that spasm and sputter near the windowpane, drinking the nectar that glows a nebulous hue. I press my lips to the wall and suck until I taste only the salt of the porous stone on my tongue.

I continue to climb and stare upward at the endless stairs above me—a double-helix ripped in two, as if the lighthouse is constructed not of stone, but of some kind of DNA and I am now a small part of it. Forever.

I consider whether I am a genetic mutation of the lighthouse.

I consider whether it is trying to eradicate me.

I consider whether I am a cancer.

I can smell the sickness in the darkness of this place. The air is getting heavier. Dense fog in my lungs. It smells of dirt, of decay—but an earthy, fungal rot, not human. Not meat. The walls are slick with dew. Patches of mold grow like tumors, feeding off of the lighthouse, illuminating a path ahead of me.

I scrape at the fuzzy spores with a jagged fingernail. The residue emanates a soft glow, like the guts of dead lightning bugs. I point upward, the residue aglow on my fingertip. My own pathetic beacon which guides me to another window.

The flora and fauna outside of the strange windows have begun to shift from traditionally avian and tree-like to subterranean. Globs of opalescent invertebrates swim, submerged in floating pools that surround the lighthouse. They swim gracefully through the liquid void, moving among the spires, leaving iridescent trails. Something else lives among them in great numbers. They pulse in the distance, peppering the depths with purple pockmarks. I am getting somewhere in the nowhere.

The messages along the walls have shifted too. They've begun to overlap in skewed, hideous lines. My name crossed out and overlaid on itself. A vile mockery of my existence. *Curtis* written in crude handwriting. *Curtis* repeated. The only word on the wall, hundreds of times in someone else's longhand.

I do not understand anything.

The farther I climb, the farther I descend.

The stairs are both a mathematical variable and a constant.

I have climbed and climbed until the soles of my shoes have been slicked as bald as the creatures outside, only for the birds to evolve into boneless, flightless skin-sacks before my eyes. I have climbed for hours. Days. Months, maybe? No. That can't be right.

But I have climbed toward the beacon, which beckons beyond, only to stop and rest along the stairs, muscles on fire, defeated; to write my notes for you.

I'm trying to help.

I'm sorry.

The last time I set foot in a library, I'd read an interesting take on the cosmology of the earth. The author believed our planet is some sort of God-egg, waiting to hatch, and everything on our planet is bacteria, trying to break through the invisible bloom of our planet, to feast on what's inside. We are all microorganisms. Think about it—even the largest of earth's animals are microscopic if viewed through the proper lens. The awful eyes are gazing down upon us. What type of fiend feeds on unborn gods?

Humans have a tendency to ask themselves, *Who am I?* But how frequently do we ask ourselves, *What am I?*

The question of metaphysical being always rests at the forefront of our minds—minds we believe to harbor an intelligence above all other creatures. A foolish belief. *Who am I? Am I a good person? What is my purpose?* While the question of our physical aspect is neglected because all one must do is look in the mirror to see the answer to the question. But how many times is the answer incorrect? The reflection shows a face. A form and figure, more or less the same as every other human on Earth. How many times is the answer lazy and ineffectual? Dig deeper. When will humans find the real answer? When will we realize that we are food for the planet we have killed—or for something else?

A voice.

Curtis.

My nails tear loose from my fingertips as I grip the stones, pulling myself up to another window. This one is broken and for the first time I am able to see outside of the lighthouse, unimpaired by the peculiar window panes.

I press my eye to the hole. A microscope.

I see shadows flit by, but not their subjects.

My hands are weak, slow from the chill of the lighthouse. I let them sag at my sides and press forward, using my hips and shoulders to place myself firmly against the hole in the window. My neck strains as I peer out. Halos of light surround the hole.

Flecks of light float through my limited view of the landscape outside of the lighthouse like dust motes. They pop like carbonated bubbles and, as they do, let out a shrill outburst that stabs at my ears. Further into the background, skinny creeping limbs jut into view and while I can't make heads or tails of their origin, they stretch and overlap as if I'm staring up into a forest canopy. They sway. They shake. They disappear.

The Being calls in cavernous grunts. The echo of its shriek reverberates throughout the nowhere. An iridescent glimmer flashes in front of the window—banks of the invertebrates skimming by like fish fleeing before a shark. The Being is close. And I am almost out of time. I have to get outside to the beacon. To salvation.

For me?

I revert my gaze from the nowhere outside of the window to the endless stairs above me. My name is scrawled continuously as above, so below, and no longer feels right anymore. The repetitious horror has stripped it of any meaning. My purpose lies within my escape into the nowhere.

As if driven by some transcendent will and the slight pull of the nowhere, I press myself into the hole in the window. My body gives, painlessly shifts to fit into the space before me. My bones creak and an intense pressure compresses my form as I walk through the irregular, chipped layers of glass.

I climb up—and out—perpendicularly onto this unfamiliar plane, as if traveling from one end of an hourglass into the other, but from a hole in the ground. The lighthouse is below me now. The hole, a speck on the surface upon which I stand. I walk around the cylindrical form below me, unable to adjust to this new, offensive gravity. My skin sagging, my joints burning from my unbearable weight. My senses focus only on the beacon, my salvation outstretched and nearly within reach.

In this time outside of time, I inhale a substance emanating from the lighthouse. A sweet nectar. An invigorating discharge. At some point, my form drifts toward the beacon. Lingering thoughts of dismantling the lenses evaporate to mist. There are no Fresnel lenses to dismantle. No glass. No.

I move toward it, and soon, my form eclipses the beacon, obscuring its pulsating glow. I trudge along and step into the light. Eggs crack beneath me, releasing a warm, yolky mire. Among the sludge, tiny frames of bone and muck squelch beneath my feet.

A vociferous peal echoes as an endless number of purple pockmarks glow throughout the depths. They cry out, hungry and impatient. A visage overtakes the horizon as it looms over its nesting ground, the Being not coming to feast, but to feed its young.

I don't wonder who I am. I don't wonder what I am. I know that I am food.

I'd laugh if my lungs could inflate, but the harsh gravity is too much to bear and I slump to the ground. Extending my arms and legs, I strain to create snow angels among the yolky slime of the unborn gods, coating myself to save the Being from knowing how humanity tastes.

Of Cedar and Sea

Ahmad Addam

"Everything is touched by the sky," my people warned me. About the sun here, always a glowing orange on a canvas of blue. About the streets, neat and perfumed with cheese and wine. About the grandeur of Byblos, the so-called Castle of Heaven. But to me, it's just a glowing, mundane city my people worship.

From the sea, I gaze at it as the boat nears the emerald coast. There's something magical in the view; Byblos still holds its fire. I indulge, just briefly, in its beauty: ember-colored tiles dancing on the water, reflecting flame-like hues. For a moment, maybe their worship makes sense. Until the land reveals itself: empty, shadowed, cloaked in quiet.

The captain stands at the prow of his ship, the sun glinting off the golden threads woven into his conical *labbadeh*, a symbol of command and seafaring pride worn by those who mastered the winds and the waves. He sounds the horn. The ship's bow curves with elegance, cutting waves like a phoenix crossing worlds. I stand at the deck's edge, eyes on the oars dipping in rhythm. Only the wind speaks, its hiss echoing from the famed mountains behind, promising the reward I seek.

The Cedars. The Peaks of Lords.

Sailors begin unloading cargo. I slip past them toward the lifeless streets. I pause to pray beside the carved horsehead on the bow, asking its blessing for my hunt. I stand steady, jasmine oil on my skin, alert. The sailors watch, but none dare block my path. The Levant knows my scythe and the many throats it has kissed.

Those who mock me will only find themselves alone, undone by their own hands.

Docking in Byblos feels like stepping into omen. Even the horsehead feels solemn, unmoved by my plea as it sails off. Ashore, a chill wraps around me like a reaper mourning a soul not yet dead. But it's mourning my defiance, the defiance of a Tyrian soul.

A few souls remain in this city. The once-vibrant scent of cheese and wine still lingers faintly in the air. As I walk, I feel their stares—startled, terrified eyes fixed on my amber abaya. Their hunger clings to the wavy black silk that flutters across the street, to the black veil shrouding my head. To them, I must seem an anomaly, an unfamiliar shadow, though we belong to the same kingdom.

I've walked through many cities in the Levant, but only here have I met such a panicked, deadly stare. As if I've been bewitched by the very mountains they call home.

Then, the sight of an alabaster castle with towering spikes breaks the mountains' haunting spell.

"The Emir," I sigh, now closer than ever to the truth behind these folklores, ones my Tyre has sent me to silence.

The castle made things much more inevitable. There are no guards. And I have never encountered an Emir in these wetlands without swords and shields, without merchants and peasants worshiping them. Most ballrooms I've visited are alive, filled with cackles and silver while peasants work like swine, foreheads glistening with sweat.

Here, the castle forecourt seeps with oddness rather than the energy of a bustling stronghold. Only trees sing to each other through the wind, birds quacking and squirrels squeaking in the bushes.

Stepping onto the entrance floor, I tuck my veil deeper into my abaya, seeking relief from the scorching heat. I stare at the gate foolishly, debating whether to knock twice or thrice. Ultimately, I turn away, considering the possibility that the Emir might be out of town, marched away with his thousand soldiers as my people had said.

I jump as the gate creaks behind me. Just inches from the darkness, I can only see the shadows of the gate tainting the floor. With a hand over my brow, I peer into the black, as if a dark star is hovering within.

Fearless, I step in.

My shadow accompanies me, bending and shifting at the threshold. So suddenly, it snaps without a sound, sealing me in a horrid darkness. I steady my heart, remembering I've survived far worse. Once I was locked in a cave with tarantulas. Another time, pushed into a cage with three lions. And once, nearly sealed with a jinni inside a bottle lamp. So how could a little darkness swamp me?

A wheezing sound screeches, not from the mountains this time, but from someone's failing lungs. I touch the hilt of my knife, ready to slit a throat. My Moallem taught me not to pray during a fight, but to stand tall like the three hills of Beirut, stronger than Alexander the Great.

In this gloomy chamber, or whatever I have trod upon, a swoosh sound echoes, followed by a dull fire as it burns. I move forward, accustomed to approaching death, until I meet a living man with croaky breaths. The little light dispels any notion of him being a ghost, a concept I never believed in anyway. Despite the dread of the moment, I can't help but giggle, as I often do when I meet my monsters.

"What has the foolish lord of Tyre sent to answer my summons?" he growls under shallow breath. A spiked crown twinkles atop his grumpy, big round head. Emirs always brag, and in this quarry city of Byblos, here is a monarch as typical as any king in the Levant.

I lower myself onto one knee, my tongue finding the words I commonly use when addressing kings and devils:

"Lord of the Snowy Mountains, Grand Emir of Byblos, and Noble of the Ember City—"

"Tsik," the Emir spits, stopping me to end my sentence. "What is a plump, pointy-breasted creature doing in my court?" he says with disgust. "I would have preferred the King of Serbia send me a hairless boy as a gift."

"Pardon my interruption, my Lord," I reply, my hand clenched into a fist, "but this plump, pointy-breasted creature fought waves and piracy to cross into your city and free it from the shaytan of the mountains."

"A wife wants to climb the rocks to slaughter the beast of the shadows? What a jinni tale!" He laughs and it doesn't provoke me to imagine his blood cooling on my knife's curve.

I push back the tip of my veil. As it flutters against my spine, I free my abaya and straighten my chin. The king struggles to maintain a steady gaze against mine.

"I see." The king bends forward, and I follow the candle as it floats from his armchair, passing over me. He clasps his hands on his belly and whispers. Perhaps to himself, or perhaps to me—

"Like a fairy tale breathing life before me." He cuts my thoughts off; the puckered expression on his face makes it hard to decipher his intentions.

"Shapash, the fisherwoman."

"Yasha, I prefer to be called," I respond, shoulders tense. I hate when men call me by a name given for their wet dreams. I'm known to be their hero. A fisherwoman that slays beasts. For me, cleansing the world and hunting monsters is as essential as breathing air. Though a bit of heavy gold or flawless gems never hurts either.

"I've heard many rumors of your extraordinary and madly heroic adventures. A king who has lived as long as I have wouldn't entertain such tales if you hadn't presented me with Seilalk Odurkr's head." He scrutinizes me, as if expecting a reaction, then leans back against his royal purple-colored cushion. "My city suffered irreparable losses due to his neurotic, barbaric behavior a decade ago."

I was merely fifteen when I chopped off Odurkr's head at sea and sealed it in honey-wax, adding it to my collection.

"He also forced my soldiers to indulge him occasionally," the king cackles, watching the candle, recalling either a profane or a poetic memory. "I truly enjoyed his company."

But the smile fades. A hateful glare replaces it, mixed with a thrilling intensity that sends a sickening chill down my gut.

"Then puff... he evaporated like a legend, leaving behind only bedtime stories."

The Lord of Tyre had dispatched a troop of soldiers to hunt Seilalk as soon as he crossed into our sea. Despite being a humble fisherwoman in Tyre, I dared many to believe in me as a fearless young huntress. My stubbornness was my ally. I concealed myself in the ship's cargo for days, enduring sickness as the ship wobbled, my stomach grumbling with little food or water. Three dawns later, the ship stopped swaying. I ventured out into the harsh wind on the muted deck. There, I saw soldiers, shorter by their heads, and Seilalk, the Barbarian of the Mediterranean, roaring in pleasure. I can't forget how his pointy toes played with a dead soldier's tooth. An intestine was strung as a necklace around his bloody, hairy chest.

I can't deny that his delight in bloodshed led to his downfall, but it was his inhumanly slim, agile body and disheveled, salt-streaked hair that gave me a chance. I crawled beneath him and slit his throat without much effort. Seilalk was like a jagged rock, yet his skin peeled like ripe berries between my teeth.

"And all kings questioned the idea of a beast plucked from the world like an orange lily, taken from his kingdom. What irony, Shapash." The Emir of Byblos remains seated on his throne, far from me, yet his breath feels hot against my cheeks as he speaks. "I loved that bastard," he admits, lips drooling, then growls bitterly, "But he snatched my kingship from my grasp as if I were a mere wimp between his sleek, oiled thighs."

He meets my gaze, peering deep. Though I find him repulsive, his eyes sparkle with a certain wisdom, even beneath his crooked, swollen nose.

"I would have ordered my ghostly worshipers to impale you with a spear and display your head above my roof. Yet... I have no soldiers in these halls. And you came to free my city. Even my cruelty found pity for it."

The Emir gestures for me to follow. My knife burns in my grip, tempting me to silence his vile tongue. But loyalty to Tyre and Phoenicia binds me. Any betrayal would strip me bare, unworthy of the Phoenix's spirit.

He leads me through another dark corridor. I stumble, blind to the castle's layout. A door ahead glows faintly. A butler pushes the Emir's wooden wheelchair, candlelight bobbing in the stale air. Byblos has no magic, only its Cedar Mountains. When the light catches the king, I finally see him. Hanging skin folds over his lap; half-grown feet drag in cotton slippers. His magenta robe cloaks bony shoulders; he is more a relic than a man.

We reach a terrace garden. A fountain sprays clear water from the mouth of a dragon-like beast, two-limbed, coiled, blackened by rain. Snow cups the mountaintop; wind roars against my face.

"Here your death starts, Shapash my girl," the Emir titters, never meeting my eyes.

"Thoban—" I try to say the name, but it shatters in my throat. Even the butler doesn't catch it. "It has many names across Libano," I manage. Is the king daring me to slay it, or memorizing my eyes before saying goodbye?

He rises. The butler gives him a staff, and he limps toward the fountain. I follow.

"I've sent thousands to the peaks. None returned. No bones, no word." His sorrow is strange coming from a king. "My strongest. Gone.

Five years ago, a plague wind poisoned half my people. I was hunting in the west."

He gazes toward the mountain. "Whispers said a demon hid in the cedars. Wives' tales, magician's fables, blasphemous to some. Dragons don't exist, they said."

But they do. And I yearn to take its head.

"Since then, the peaks stay white. The wind never stops. Even winter fears our skies."

The king clasps my hands. His touch is warm, trembling, human. No son, I imagine, has known this part of him.

"I'm not begging, Yasha of the South. But even the cruelest king has a heart somewhere inside."

He's not weeping. He's asking for vengeance, the reason he looks straight into me.

"Restore my Byblos."

Alone in the dense, shady pine forest that thickens as I ascend toward the mountains, I face the drought that birthed wildness in the cold. Thoban, the monster I long to slay, hisses with sharp and vehement intensity, its breath deadly. It stands as a rival, an opponent I'm determined to scratch off my list.

The Emir has only offered ghost soldiers to assist me. The city is now inhabited mostly by elders and witches who speak of the creature, making it an even more formidable challenge. I tighten my veil around my collar, ice gnawing at my chest despite the wool coat draped over my shoulders. It proves useless in the shaggy woods, where snow and slippery soil greet me both above and below the crown of pine trees.

The higher I climb, the colder it becomes, numbing my fingertips. Here, the pines are gone, replaced by thick layers of cedars. So, I follow the sun, which seems to flee from the mountains, slowly descending and beckoning dusk to quell its fear. But prayers are futile, and surrender is never an option.

To brighten my name in the South ever more, I welcome death as a sister, refusing to be spat upon. I was born a heroine, and that spirit will endure until the end of time.

Amidst the tangled foliage, I stumble upon a lost, jeweled temple, now wreathed with vines and grass. Once dedicated to a god, a new mosaic now adorns its weakened walls, a depiction of the dragon-like creature of the Cedar, its straight yellowish irises evoking memories of the jinns I had sealed in Solomon's castle.

Born alone on the hot, beachy coast of Libano, without a father to protect me or a mother to nurture me, I married the sea to become a fisherwoman and survive. The dream of becoming a huntress arose when I learned of the rewards offered for such deeds. From poverty, I had toiled and dived beside the monsters of the Mediterranean Sea, transforming myself into what I have matured into. Over time, my passion for rewards diminished, and the lust for journeys and assassinations ignited and grew.

Out of nowhere, the cedar trees stop growing as I reach the topmost crest of the mocking mountain. Only a few trees tower from the solid, craggy rocks, their spiky crowns gray and lethal. Their roots intertwine like serpents slithering across the solid ground beneath me. In the darkest of darknesses, I try to listen to the timbers singing, sobbing for air and water, but all I hear is the eerie hissing of the supersonic winds.

But the whistling breeze stops flowing when it clashes with a passage shaped into a cave.

I venture into the cave, and to my surprise, the inside is brighter, sunnier than the foreign night. Perhaps some soldiers sought refuge in the mountains, too afraid to flee, too afraid of the night. They might have preferred famine over confronting the freak, or whatever devil might appear to peel the flesh from their bones.

I follow the light, yellow in hue, dimmer than the sun but harder than gold.

A growl? No... a whisper? It is neither.

A purr echoes in the cave and my heart races like never before. Blood pumping, tongue frozen, skin numb.

"At last, a worthy set of bones between my fangs." A shadow slashes across the ground, and a rattle halts my next step.

Before I can catch the stray eyes of the demon watching me, the living thing lashes its tail, slamming me against the wall. My back cracks, and I tumble to the ground. With my arm shielding my face, the beast assaults me with a noxious stink that punches my nose.

Struggling to breathe, I suddenly catch what caused my heart to skip: a cat pacing closer, its eyes glittering on and off in the yellowish light. Its hard, wrinkled tail lashes behind it, playfully circling a rat scurrying into its territory. Its four clawed paws screech beneath its shadow.

"I taste fear... with a hint of courage. Rare to encounter in a year. Juicy blood with jasmine buds. A delicious deer," the beast snarls.

I slide my knife out, one arm cupping my nose, knees buckling beneath me. No creature would offend me. I swore it in my blood. Swore it to the horsehead of Phoenicia.

The snake gives a series of cackles through its forked tongue.

"Men desire me most. What more, warriors who dare wrestle with my dearest claws?"

Its tail sways in delight, poised to slough my skin and suck my blood.

I preserve silence, hands clenched tightly around my knife's handle. The dragon-cat hisses, laughing in a crescendo mingled with its hot, foul breath.

"What iron can rip through my skin? What rewards have driven you to handle such sin?"

Without a word, I slice through the wind, slip under the beast, and deliver a deep cut into its gut. The dragon-cat hisses. As I crash into the wall, following its long, fluffy tail, I first think it is dying, but then I realize it is laughing.

My prized metal betrays me, snapping in two and leaving me defenseless.

The cat flicks its devilish eyes toward me and looms overhead.

"No man has dared touch me," it growls, yellow irises blinding me.

It sniffs over me, its snout grazing my pale cheek, the veil over my frizzy head fluttering free. It stares, scanning me like an owl, from hair to toes. A short growl, then a grin.

"Big breasts with gravely brawny arms. Guileless eyes and a reckless sword. A woman came to bring about my downfall, to slit my throat. Odd, isn't it?"

"Embarrassed, aren't you?" I finally find my words after an endless hunt on my tongue. Every creature had once sniggered at me for having no toys between my legs, before I ended them.

"Opposite," the beast snarls.

The craving for blood on its grumpy face vanishes. Its claws slide back into its paws. I rise, knees shaking, shocked by the turn.

"Won't you drink my blood and taste my flesh between your jaws?" I ask, stepping back.

"Maybe," it replies, curling its tail around itself, and I shiver, pressing harder on my broken knife.

There's a trick. There is always a trick.

"Are you here to taunt me, like the men did?" it asks.

"Are you trying to humiliate me because I wield a sword, with pointy breasts and a womb?" I snap.

The dragon-cat tilts its head toward the mouth of the cave, its gaze distant.

"They call me by many names. Thoban, Arassas, Hakirat el-Hay, Manfakh el-Nar, Zoulayma... and more."

"They call me by many names, too. Shameful. Weakling. Veiled."

"I was once a woman," the creature says, as if recalling its past life, as a human, as a woman. "Civilly degraded men christened us with many names, whether we were beautiful like your eyes or ugly like mine. Brave like yours or cursed like mine."

"Is that why you're wiping out an entire village?" I say, trying to play its game.

"The system deserves a shameful, deserving death. The wheel deserves those venomous breaths. Everything in this universe deserves darkness... and horrible Seth," the cat murmurs, laying its furry head down as if to sleep.

"Am I not a threat to you?" I press, tongue dry.

"It rests on what you're choosing," it replies, one eye half open.

"Are you mocking me?" I raise my voice, and the mountain screeches and trembles.

"You are a huntress, sailing from coast to coast for the sake of stupid stability in Phoenicia. Balancing our seas and mountains from beasts that might destabilize that centralized, disgraceful system," the creature says, reading my thoughts as if I've lost control of them.

"Don't you prefer to share power to ensure balance? Don't you crave to end things without civil cities pointing at you, for not being a man?"

My veil's fame has spread across the Eastern cities, and I am still considered a ghastly, rebellious woman: a taboo.

The beast glances back at me with both eyes before whispering: "Don't you wish to be invincible?"

Yes. I wish it dearly.

"Then... you have freed me at last. And Byblos shall see darkness no more."

The beast smiles, and with a hiss, it pounces over me and bites me.

Shock waves run through my blood when Thoban bites me, but it isn't suffering that overwhelms me. Instead, it is a fragment of pleasant tickling, mixed with a dull headache. I realize it's the dragon's memories entering me: when it was once mortal. A petite, attractive woman with black wavy hair and skin as radiant as moonlit snow. She had a son and a spouse, and her heart shimmered with love.

Love.

In a finger snap, everything was stripped from her.

Love twisted into rage and malice.

The harmony she once knew vanished.

She was Fariha, the grace of Byblos, a dweller of the beautiful city, its ash houses adorned with fireworks each night, its moonlit evenings, and a sky that transitioned from summer to autumn, calling for winter before spring.

Fariha. Torn from her husband and son, torn from love and everything she held dear. They were humble peasants, poor and overtaxed by the wickedest king of the brutal city.

Disgusted with her existence, Fariha vanished into the mountains, where she encountered another creature, another folklore, another girl with a terrible story.

I open my eyes, and the darkness turns into color.

My hands feel heavy with claws. My tongue sprouts jasmine.

Should I end up like the other women: seeking vengeance, crushing childhoods, and terrifying lives under many nicknames?

I hold power now, thick in my blood. I pour it into authority, adopting a new talent to fulfill my endless, exhausting purpose as a huntress. Darkness has never been my greatest fear.

I pile a layer of fat from the Emir's body under my paw, ensuring he keeps breathing. I have snatched him in the night, punished him for what he did to many women. Every time he spills blood, I blow blood back into his heart. I mend his wounds after every cut, enforcing pain, never allowing him to forget the taste of his cruelty.

I growl over him and stare at the moon outside, glinting on the peaks, watching the music and festivals. Never timid again from the crests of Byblos.

An end to my adventures in the seas.

A dawn to the downfall of the cruelest kings.

The Unbroken Circle

MJ HUNTSGOOD

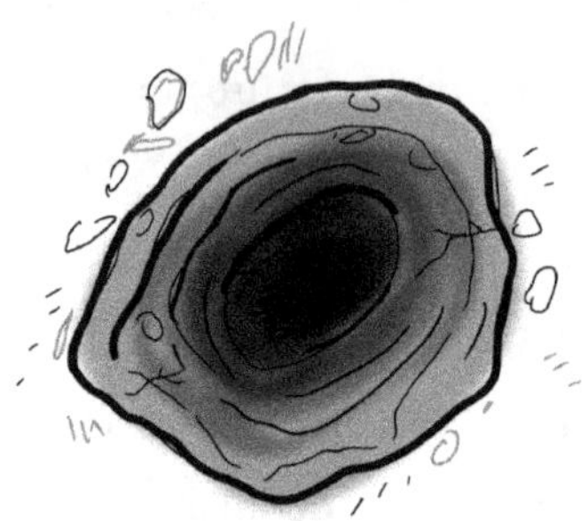

UNBELIEVERS ARE FED TO the Hole.

No one is sure how deep the Hole is, or how it came to be in the center of the barn, but that is where the town meets now. Every Sunday for church, every Wednesday for their town meetings.

Every time there is a sign that an Unbeliever is going to strike.

"I say it was Horace," a big voice booms, picking at the hole in his molar. "I ain't never trusted him, not since he was a wee thing. Full of that Unbelief."

"Now Jameson, ain't no good blaming your brother," Father Arnold says from the front of the barn, the only member of the town illuminated by candlelight. "Ain't pretty business, these dead animals. Ain't pretty business when it becomes more, neither."

"I hate this," the woman with the baby in her arms says. "I just don't think we should do it."

"You saw the cow carcass, Sarah, same as the rest of us." Father Arnold lifts up his flyswatter and smacks one that lands on the table. *Smack.*

Father Arnold does not relent. "We have the evening to figure it out." When the first decayed corpse is found, it's only a matter of time before the Unbeliever takes a life. The town only has so much time.

The town is so far away from everyone else.

Caroline stands up, her wiry body flapping about like a dish towel on the line. "We ain't got no Unbelievers in this town. We're a good town. You know that. I don't see why we're all sitting here around the Hole, ready to toss someone in here to their death."

There is a murmur of agreement.

"Careful of that door handle there, Caroline," Father Arnold says, gesturing to the trap door obscured by the darkness. "Don't need you breaking your neck."

Before the Hole, the trap door was where Unbelievers went until they repented. Now, there is no repentance. There is only the Hole.

Father Arnold says it is better this way.

"You remember what happened the last time we didn't work out who was the Unbeliever?" Father Arnold says. "What happened to the children?"

Everyone remembers.

Another fly lands on the table. *Smack.*

"There are always Unbelievers among us," Caroline says. "Even when we work out that we've got them all, there are always more. Don't that worry nobody but me?"

"It's 'cause that Unbelief is like a disease. It spreads from one to another." Horace spits. "Makes you forget why we're all here in the first place."

He peers down the thick, root-encrusted sides of the Hole. There is probably a bottom, somewhere past the mud and the darkness.

"You'd know all about that, wouldn't you, Horace?" Jameson sneers. His teeth are jagged and sharp. His wits? Not so much.

"Why don't you just shut yer trap like Pa-Paw always said you should?" Horace spits again, a thick coagulation of tobacco. "'Cause he always knew you were worth nothin'."

The two men rise and members of the congregation step in between them.

Father Arnold gets to his feet. "If you two can't get yourselves right, I'll feed you both to the Hole myself. We've got— " *Smack!* "—precious little time to figure out our Unbeliever amongst us, and I'm afraid we're gonna have to work together to figure out who it is."

Caroline sits primly on a bale of hay, while Sarah begins to nurse. Horace produces another bag of tobacco and Jameson picks at his fingernails with a knife. The rest of the town snuggles together like a rat king, its bound tail keeping it warm and safe and destined for death.

"Now." Father Arnold steps out from behind the table placed in front of the Hole.

"We have one dead cow, killed in the typical fashion of the Unbelievers. Slit throat, open gullet. Can see that by the knife marks, even if we ain't got no meat on the bones left." He pauses. "There's always meat on the bones left. Concerning it's different this time." *Smack.* "Let's go through all the town members one at a time. Find out where y'all was last night."

Sarah shifts on the hay. "Well, I'll tell you, Father Arnold, neither me nor my husband could be an Unbeliever. We're too devout. And seeing as we both been up with little Ellie here all night, there's no way we could have done away with that cow."

"Here's some shit," Horace snaps. "Unbelievers, the both of ya. 'Twere Jimmy's cow and you hate Jimmy, and you could have taken turns with Ellie."

"Maybe Ellie's an Unbeliever," Jameson pipes up.

"On the *tit,* Jameson?" Father Arnold snaps.

"Well, I don't know, Father Arnold, why don't you *tell* us how we're supposed to work this out?"

The town murmurs in agreement. When this happens, they always follow behind Father Arnold. He always figures out who the Unbeliever is, and the killings always stop. It is a dark, sad night. There is crying. There is pain.

You are, of course, among them.

The Unbeliever.

At this point, you're not even sure what you're supposed to Believe in, but asking would give yourself away. Belief is all that matters.

And you lost it.

"Ain't nobody leaving." Father Arnold circles the Hole. "Horace locked the barn door and I ain't opening it until we get some answers."

"Weren't me," Horace says, straightening up.

"So you keep sayin'," Jameson snaps. "Go on. Tell us where you was."

Horace's eyes flick to Caroline. She shakes her head.

Opportunity.

You tell Father Arnold that Horace was with you. Your eyes catch Horace's. He's dumber than a box of rocks, but he's your friend. You go fishing together. You hunt.

He knows what you are, though. You're *sure* of it.

Smack. This time it's Jimmy, the owner of the cows in question. He's been sitting in the corner this whole time, silent. He crushes the fly with his hand.

"God*damn,* Arnold, why does this barn have so many flies?"

Father Arnold lets the air out of his nose. "Jimmy, it's August and you know how them horse flies get."

"Not around the Hole, they don't." Jimmy's voice is deep like a graveyard and unsettles the whole congregation.

You ask Father Arnold how we know that these animal deaths are Unbelievers and not someone on the outside trying to tear the town apart, considering this is the fifth Unbeliever this year and it's only August. That's a lot for such a small town.

There is a murmur of agreement and you feel the warmth and protection of the town surrounding you.

You are liked by the town. It feels good.

Smack! Another fly meets its end by Jimmy's hand and Father Arnold straightens up. "I don't think someone would come that far to hurt us. And there ain't no outsider that knows about the Hole and Belief. Seein' as I didn't tell nobody."

No one would. You look down into the Hole.

The Hole looks back into you.

"So where was you, Caroline?" Father Arnold asks. "Ain't nothing that can't be said in this town, but it needs to be said here."

"I was at home," Caroline says.

"No you weren't," Jameson snaps. "It's her, I said it!"

Caroline spins on him. "And where was you?"

"I was *at home* where you weren't."

"Alone?"

"Yeah."

"How can you prove *I* weren't home alone?"

"Cause you *weren't!*"

Father Arnold hits the table with his hand. "Shut it! I'm liable to throw both of ya into the Hole! Now one of you is lying!"

One of them is and you know which one.

Father Arnold steps up to the two of them. "This ain't just about where you *was*. It's about *Belief.*"

Belief. Last week you sat on the rock near the train track and watched the smoke rise from the new aluminum factory in the distance. It streamed out like cotton from a torn-up pillow. A pillow, pressed down and *down*. It was so distant.

"Ain't no sign of all that cow meat," Sarah says. "That means it's either been et already, which I'm gon' doubt, or it's somewhere near. Figure out where it be—"

Jameson picks at his fingernails, thick black gunk dropping onto the dirt floor. "I still say it were my brother."

Caroline is up faster than a chicken after feed. She stands between the two men. "Now, I won't have you talking about Horace this way, Jameson, I've been putting up with it this whole meeting. Everybody in the town *knows* what this is about! He ain't no Unbeliever, he's your brother!"

Jameson's eyes burn. "You got something to say, Caroline?"

"Ain't no good being this angry, James, it was months ago," she hisses at him.

"Yeah, and I ain't got the stench of the two a' you outta my bed yet." Jameson leans back against one of the beams.

Father Arnold pipes up. "We ain't got time for your marital problems, y'all. We gonna have to throw someone in the Hole today. Nobody's imaginings or fantasies gettin' in the way. Someone *real.*"

Jimmy nods real slow. "You sure bent on ending a life today no matter what, Arnold."

There is silence in the barn for a long moment. The candle is the only light, casting long, thick shadows across the Hole, across the rafters. You hear the flutter of a few bats brave enough to stay in the barn with the Hole. No other animals dare to.

Animals don't approach the Hole.

You actually don't know the connection between the Hole and animals at all. But you are drawn to cows. To their necks. To their throats.

And you have been this way for *years*.

"How we done know that Unbeliever killed them animals?" Horace asks, spitting again. All eyes turn to him. "He—or she—be drawing a lot of attention to themself."

"It's what happens," Father Arnold explains. "There is an animal, and then there is a person. They start out slow."

"You always catch them though, don't you?" Sarah says. "You figure out who among us ain't got the faith and toss them right there in that Hole. It's like they ain't been causing no problems until they kill that first animal."

Father Arnold lifts a finger. "Remember Sally Hawes."

You remember Sally Hawes. The open window, the thrashing.

"Yeah, that poor little girl, smothered in her bed," Jameson says. "Couldn't work out if it was the Unbeliever or the Hole that did it. Or if it were because we didn't want to follow you."

Caroline moves herself subtly between Father Arnold and you. "I don't think we should hunt an Unbeliever this time. That cow weren't worth that much to Jimmy, don't you think?"

Jimmy grunts.

"What are you all saying?" Father Arnold snaps.

You rise.

You tell him that you're all saying the same thing. That you're tired of the flies in the room. Flies are attracted to rotting things.

Maybe it's time you saw what was under the floor.

The town looks at Father Arnold, eyes wide as a Carolina moon.

"I don't know what you mean," he says.

You believe him, but the town doesn't. You have reason to. It wasn't easy last night, getting into this barn. The Hole moaned at you.

Now, the *town* is bent on solving the mystery.

Jameson moves to the trap door and grips the o-ring on the floor. Flies pour out. The rotted smell of meat fills the air.

Horace steps down the ladder. He comes up with a pillow. Sally Hawes' pillow.

They turn.

On Father Arnold.

One word comes from the town's lips. All of them speak it in unison. They clasp your hand and pull you with them as they circle Father Arnold and drive him towards the Hole, towards the endless fall.

"Unbeliever!"

Father Arnold thrashes in their arms like a child in a bed. He kicks like a cow. He is lifted out of the safety of his friends and thrown and falls—

And they pray.

You pray with them.

A fly lands on your face.

Flies are attracted to rotten things.

The Eagles are Nesting at Pheasant Run

Brooke Lanier

IN A BREAKING WORLD, on a quiet street, within an unassuming brick building whose walls are lined with thousands of glass timers, the soft hiss of falling sand fills the ears of Nobody.

Nobody is, after all, already walking down the hallway, heels clicking with the confidence of someone who has walked the same path for a millennium. Despite this, the tiles remain in pristine condition. Though earthquakes follow blinding flashes outside as the world wages war on itself, the library is undisturbed, without so much as a quiver in its foundation.

She flips a laminated card between her long fingers, marred by a cross stitch of white lines—years of paper cuts. It is for a worthy cause, though. Nobody would bleed herself dry, paper cut by paper cut, if it meant that the library could continue.

The card is blank on one side, the other detailed with a title, name, and duration in neat cursive. The duration on the card, of course, corresponds to the time frame in which it takes every grain of sand to pass from the upper bulb to the lower bulb. This card's timer is nearly finished.

Nobody pivots into the first room she reaches, lush floral rugs now dampening the sounds of her movement. She glances down at the card again. It also refers to the location of a book within the library, and this one leads her down rows of wooden bookcases lined with clothbound hardcover novels. Some look brand new, while others appear so worn she'd only dare touch them with a fresh pair of gloves.

The shelves gather dust as she continues farther down the aisles. Eventually, she reaches the section where each book's plot spans seventeen years. Here, only one book waits for her attention, its cover the palest blue. Nobody verifies that the title, *An Exploration into Ornithology,* matches the card's secondary field. Nobody listens hard, but if any bird calls between the pages, it is too hushed beneath the waves of falling sand from the tower down the hall.

Carefully, Nobody cradles the book in her arms and leaves the room. At the other end of the hall, the doorway expands into a clean lobby, though all Nobody can see from here is the coat rack overflowing with heavy coats and gas masks. Nobody heads in that direction, barely reacting to the lingering smell of ozone that seeps through the crack at the bottom of the front door, but stops when she reaches the next door, its dark wood carved with intricate chrysanthemums and grains of wheat. It pushes open without so much as a creak. Inside, the walls are lined with thick tapestries, the woven fantastical depictions moving softly within the confines of their edges. Nobody swings a painting from the wall, its hinges well oiled, to reveal a keypad, and with the press of a few buttons, the knights and castles reweave themselves into scenes of avian menageries. She hides the keypad once more, and the digital tapestry's pixels soften until they look no more than stitches of fabric.

She places the novel on a wooden pedestal in the center of the chamber and uses a golden clasp to hold it open to its last page before settling onto the edge of a soft armchair, its match facing hers on the other side of the pedestal. Nobody refers to the card once more before placing it next to the book.

Nobody isn't sure which she notices first: the slight quieting of the sand that accompanies the end of a timer, or the soft ripple across the white page in front of her.

Nobody crosses her legs, folds her hands, and waits. "Sweet waking, Leigh Unel."

The ripples' frequency increases, blurs of gray against the aged white paper, until finally, a shade turns into a shadow, and that shadow turns into a silhouette, and then Leigh emerges like a developing image on light-sensitive film.

Words cover her skin like bruises, their frequency of use in the novel determining the boldness of the font, the lines of words like "I," "and," and "the" so thick they are nearly unreadable, though Nobody can still tell.

The words fade as Leigh comes into focus, laugh lines by her eyes barely defined, just a hint of them really, even as a beatific smile spreads.

The blissful peace will fade too—everything does. As Leigh returns to reality, so will her real-life memories. Nobody has seen the smiles melt away countless times. The eyes dull and darken. The fists clench as they remember why they sought solace in the first place.

The library is a respite, but it is not a destination. Every patron leaves eventually.

Nobody stays.

And maybe if she spends more time with the patrons as they wake, she'll feel their loss when she is alone again. Perhaps if Nobody ever slows down, she'll have more time to acknowledge her own emotions, but as it currently stands, she has mere minutes before the next patron reaches the end of their book.

So, she waits for each one to blink the words from their eyes. She briefs them on any news they missed during the duration of their read, though the details blur in the final scenes of a dying world. Then she ushers them to the door.

Gravity must feel different in books, or perhaps it's just the sensation of being paper thin, because there's always a moment where each person staggers or shifts while developing, and suddenly Nobody is standing to guide them to the armchair opposite hers.

Leigh sinks into the armchair and nods, prompting Nobody to return to her own. "How long has it been?" She works her jaw as though the sensation of speaking is foreign.

"Seventeen years."

Leigh nods, dropping her eyes. "I feel older, somehow. Tired, at the very least. Is that normal?"

"That is the word fog. It will pass. Your physical age has not changed."

Leigh inspects the backs of her hands, flipping them in her lap before nodding in confirmation.

"Some patrons find it comforting to discuss what they read."

Leigh pulls the book into her hands and traces the worn spine. "I feel like I'm still there, still walking down Pheasant Run. The trees aren't yet budding, and these giant nests of twigs and sticks wave in the wind near the highest branches. Six more weeks, and I swear I'll hear chirping."

She closes her eyes as if she's concentrating on the sounds around her, trying to hear the birds.

"Chirping?"

"Do you remember the spring?"

"The concept is," Nobody searches for the correct phrase, *"familiar,* yes, but abstract at best."

"My favorite part of the book," Leigh reaches to trace the spine, "was springtime, and the eagles had begun to nest. They're together, diving and swirling in pairs. The sight of their wings as they glided down to the trees: I'll never forget it." She holds her arms out at her sides and sways slightly.

Gently as she can, Nobody explains, "Unfortunately, like a dream, your experiences in *An Exploration into Ornithology* will dissipate as time passes." Patrons never seem to remember the introductory speech when they wake, but Nobody has endless patience.

Leigh looks crestfallen. She whispers, "If I could hold onto the sight forever, I would," before burying her head in her hands.

"Forever is a long time." Nobody knows that forever feels like shifting sands and sounds like falling spirits.

"When you're facing oblivion, nothing is long enough." Leigh's voice is muffled behind her palms. "Unless the world happened to fix itself while I was checked in?" She raises her head to search Nobody's expression, but Nobody is well-versed in composing her face.

Nobody begins with a question. "Have you heard of the phrase 'nuclear winter' before?"

Leigh frowns. Considers this.

There is never an easy way to tell someone their world is ending, but Nobody does not have time to ease patrons into their fate. "The sun will never shine its rays on this world's inhabitants again."

There are not five stages of grief for this: it is one crescendo that builds until the pressure becomes too much. Nobody expects the normal reaction: tears, screaming, tantrums. But Leigh does not react.

Nobody shifts to sit on her twitching fingers instead, unnerved by the lack of response. Leigh holds steady, staring at the wall.

Silence pervades the space, not heavy or suffocating, just present.

When Leigh finally speaks, it is not to ask about friends, or family, or money, or any of the things patrons commonly mourn. "And the birds?"

"Pardon?"

"What happened to the birds?"

"Those who weren't killed in the initial blasts, or choked by the ashes, perished from..." She trails off, watching a single tear meander down Leigh's pale cheeks. Most patrons cry for themselves.

"My father loved them," Leigh whispers. "He'd take me walking down Pheasant Run in early spring, pointing up at the giant nests on the tops of bare trees. 'See up there, Leigh Bug?' he'd say. 'The eagles are nesting!' And I'd nod and crane my neck for a glimpse of an eggshell, but I was always too short to see. He'd scoop me up for a better view, all too ready to carry both our worlds on his shoulders."

"Is that why you picked that particular book to check into? To feel closer to him?"

She laughs, a rough sound. "You know, I can't even recall his face anymore, yet I remember how he spoke of the birds. I always thought I'd do the same for my own child eventually."

Nobody nods, though she does not understand. "All patrons come to the library to relive the past or experience lost dreams. For many, they are one and the same."

Leigh clears her throat. "And you? Why do you stay?"

Nobody frowns. She has never been asked that before. Eventually, she responds. "Someone must bear witness to the end."

"That sounds awfully lonely."

"It is necessary."

"Why?"

Nobody twitches with discomfort. Here is the opportunity to speak the words she has never said, and yet they have grown so heavy she can feel them choking her: because otherwise, all the dreams and hopes and fears that everyone in this world experienced mean nothing, and this end does not mean anything. It's just the end. She opens her mouth to respond just so, but Nobody realizes that the background sound is quieter.

Another timer has run out of sand.

"It is time to go," Nobody says, rising to her feet in one graceful motion. "Another patron needs me."

"Of course." Leigh jolts up from her chair and swipes the wetness from her cheek. They both sweep into the hall and Leigh shuffles forward, her scuffing sneakers at odds with the heel clicks that echo against the tiles.

"Can I come back to experience the memory again?"

"Patrons do not return."

The shuffling slows, Leigh's movement barely a whisper above the falling sands. "Perhaps I will be the first," she mutters.

Nobody could correct her, but time, after memory, is the last commodity at the end of the world. For Leigh, it has run out. Nobody guides her to the lobby where the curtains are drawn to hide the skies dark with ash. Drawn is gentler on the patrons, despite having no effect on the state of the outside world.

At the front door, Leigh pauses, stopping Nobody with a light hand on her shoulder. "How do I face oblivion?"

Nobody ponders this. "The same way you face forever, I suppose."

Save for the timers, their shifting sands barely a whisper in their ears, the room is quiet. Something like recognition passes between them.

When Leigh finally moves, she does so alone.

The simple brass doorknob is cold to the touch, as metal typically is. Leigh inhales deeply. On the exhale, she turns the knob and pulls the wooden door open slowly, as though it is heavier than she expected.

With a final glance back at the now-empty lobby, she walks across the threshold.

Roots

HARPER KINSLEY

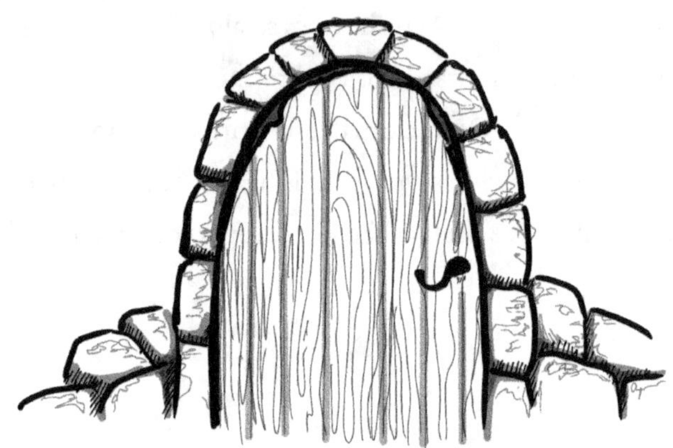

THE FOREST HAS MY son and I am taking him back.

Decaying leaves crumble and mist parts beneath my feet with each step I take. The air around me is thick and heavy with the smell of earth and the cold dampness of the coming rain. Overhead I hear the call of birds and cicadas, an evening symphony for the golden, late autumn light that breaks through the clouds and the leaves where it can. Some might call it serene. I might agree with them, if I didn't hate this place so much.

There is a ghost story about the ruins in the depths of Blackwood Forest. Crumbling walls that support a worn, mahogany door. Supposedly, the door contains an enchanted passageway, and passing through it takes you to the land of spirits.

But I know better. What waits inside is much, much worse.

Armed with an aluminum bat slung across my back and a flashlight in hand, I head due north, if my compass is correct. My phone doesn't work out here. It's stifling to feel so cut off from the world when all I want to do is call home and tell Ella that I love her. That I understand why she's mad at me, even if she says she isn't. That it's okay if she doesn't love me anymore, because I wouldn't love me either.

Even if she hasn't said it. She doesn't have to. I just know.

Ella. My anchor. Without her voice, my thoughts continue to funnel down the spiral.

What if I'm too late?

What if I can't find the ruins?

Do I even know what I'm doing?

I stop, breaking free of my ruminations just in time to see the ruins.

Before me stand the ruins I've been searching for. I expect some huge, grand thing—like the entrance to a great cathedral or mausoleum—but it can't be much taller than me. Time and the forest have claimed the weathered gray stones, covered the gate in lively, green moss and streaks of dirt. The wind stills and the forest quiets as my eyes land on the door. Decrepit planks of dark wood, loosely hanging on black metal hinges attached to an archway. A portal to another space.

All I have to do now is take hold of the handle and step through. But I find myself frozen. Gods know what's waiting for me on the other side. Ice spreads from my chest, through my arms and to my fingertips. Like when I see a knife in the kitchen and fear I've driven it into my wife's back. Like when I hear a noise in the middle of the night and convince myself I've endangered the family by not locking the door, despite knowing I've done it. An anxiety so anchored inside that I itch until I get up to check.

Two times.

Or five.

Sometimes more.

"Mama?"

My attention snaps to the door once again, but no one's there. Still, I heard him. Jonah's voice, distant, but clear.

And foolishly, I dare to hope.

I slide my compass into my pocket, then I grasp the door's iron handle. It's bone-cold against my already frozen fingers. Enough to make me stop and reconsider.

Jonah isn't the first to go missing. The forest claimed a group of teenagers three years ago and the officer who went looking for them. Before that, it took someone's wandering father who left home without a word, and his adult child as well. If I step through this door, I may never come back. I may leave Ella without a wife. After having just lost our son.

A memory flashes in my mind. The look of devastation on her face when they told us Jonah had disappeared. And I know what I must do.

I pull on the handle, and the door opens.

No one has returned from the forest to tell what to expect on the other side. The stories only warn of its dangers, not what lies in wait or how to escape.

But when I step through, nothing changes.

The same evening light—now approaching twilight—slips through the trees, and the wind passes through the red and brown leaves above me. The same heavy air surrounds me, and the ground beneath me is littered with leaves and branches.

This can't be right.

I step back through the threshold. Then step through. The forest remains the same.

"No," I hiss. "No, no, no." I try again.

Still nothing. My heart rate rises as I repeat the process over and over, throwing the door open and crossing through.

"Let me in!" I yell, unsure if anyone—any*thing*—can actually hear me.

When I enter the gate again, my foot gives way, and I collapse onto the ground with a hard thud. My hands slide beneath me, but I catch myself on my elbows and knees, my face almost planted in the dirt. I feel every inch of the mud on my hands, my fingers, under my nails, on my clothes, the dampness of the ground through the knees of my pants. It's stifling, a vice-like cage consuming my skin.

I can't get up.

I can't get up.

Open your eyes, I tell myself. *Open your damn eyes.*

But I can't.

Yes. You can. You have to.

So I do. I pry them open and then slowly push myself back to my knees. I see just how much mud covers me, and I shudder. Bugs. Sickness. Disease. The safety alarm screams in my head, the need to remove the contaminant. But I force myself to wipe the tears away from my eyes, carefully using the clean hem of my shirt. I breathe in. Out.

Then I turn my attention in front of myself once more.

The mist is up to my ankles now, a thick cover that makes it difficult to see much of anything on the forest floor. Despite my better judgment, I reach down, fishing around for the flashlight I dropped just seconds ago. After a minute of searching, my fingers brush against the cold metal and I lean forward to take it.

As I do, the smallest glint of light from the ground catches my eye. I halt when I see what it is.

A bright red race car I would know anywhere.

Jonah is here.

"I'm coming for you," I whisper, then snatch the car from the ground and slide it securely into my pocket.

I stand, feeling the weight of the baseball bat once more. It's slung over my shoulder in a sleeve made of cheap, plastic fabric. I don't dare hold it in my hand. Not yet, at least. I don't want to use it at all. The only way I can handle my intrusive thoughts is knowing I'm not capable of violence.

But I will do what it takes to save Jonah.

I do my best to brush the filth from my clothes, but even when there's nothing left sticking to me, I feel every place the mud has touched me like Lady Macbeth's stain. My free hand, the one not holding the flashlight, clenches in and out of a fist as I attempt to flick the non-existent dirt from it. I need to wash it. I should have brought hand sanitizer, if nothing else.

As I head deeper within, the trees grow denser and the light begins to fade. I can barely make out the path just ahead of me after a while, and I trip once or twice on tree roots as a result. Eventually, I turn on the flashlight, which is one of those industrial ones, complete with a metal finish and an LED as efficient as a modern headlight. It's enough to help me find a way forward, at least.

I slip my compass out of my pocket and glance down at it to check my heading. But the compass no longer points in one direction. Instead, it wildly whips back and forth, stopping for just seconds before whirling around in random circles. Whatever this place is, it doesn't want me to leave when this is over. And it certainly doesn't want me to find my son.

Fine. If the forest wants to fight, I'll fight back.

Reaching into my other pocket, I pull out my multipurpose tool. I've never owned anything like this before, and I debated even buying one at all. But in the end, I decided I could withstand the visions for the sake of self defense. For the sake of survival. Carefully, I free the knife blade and make sure it's firmly in place before turning to a tree where I can see a notch in the bark. I shove the knife into the notch and pull down as hard as I can.

The bark gives. I wrap my fingers under it and pull.

When it snaps, I stumble back, but this time I manage to catch myself before I fall.

My breathing shallows when I feel something wet beneath my palms.

I watch as something dark and red and viscous flows from the tree. Like sap. Like blood. Then I realize it's under my fingers, attached to the bark I've just wrenched free. I cry out and release it, and it falls to the ground where I can see the liquid oozing out onto the grass. The substance runs down the side of the tree as well, from the place where I've created an open wound.

Deep breaths, I tell myself. I squint my eyes shut, breathing in and out, concentrating on the filling and emptying of my lungs. But no matter how much I wipe my fingers on the sides of my pants, I still feel it. Even after I can't see it anymore. I wish I had somewhere—any-where—to wash my hands, even some dirty forest stream. Not that it would matter by now. I could wash them a thousand times and still feel the residue of whatever it is I've just touched.

Finally, I open my eyes. The tree has formed a sort of dark scab, thick and shining with whatever's clotted over it. I tentatively shine my flashlight at it, and to my slightest relief, it catches the light just enough for me to see it. At least I'll have something to lead me back home when all this is done.

"Mama!"

His voice again. Closer now. I can make out a direction this time and I follow it, knowing full well that the forest may be leading me towards my doom. But I have nothing else to go on, so I'll follow it anyway.

Still, I grasp the flashlight even tighter.

My pace quickens. The cloud of what once was mist has risen to my waist and thickened to a proper fog. I take longer strides, stumbling every so often, but I start to learn the forest's tricks. Roots sticking out of the ground, fallen logs obstructing the way forward. I step carefully, leap over the trees. Every so often I cut another piece of bark to mark a path for myself, squirming as the tree oozes again each time.

But as I venture further in, the forest grows more frantic. A shriek, like the squeal of metal and the cry of an animal, echoes through the forest and I hesitate for a moment before continuing. If I didn't know better, I'd have mistaken it for a deer. Or maybe even Ella's screams. At one point, I think I see something in the trees—a passing shadow in the shape of something animal-like. I keep my distance. Chasing shadows in the forest is how you get killed, after all.

I'm hyper-aware of the rustle of the bushes now. Every sound makes me jump, heightening my skyrocketing anxiety. What if I'm too late? The knife in my pocket suddenly feels heavy. I should have been more careful, I should have thought harder. My assault on the trees will lead to Jonah's death. I've angered the forest, and it will destroy me.

Jonah's voice cuts through the fog, now up to my shoulders, threatening to submerge me entirely. "Mama!"

"Jonah?" I shout.

I can't help it. His voice is so close now, so clear. There's no way it's in my head. *I'm almost there. I'm going to find you.*

I have to hurry.

I walk. Then I run.

I can feel him, some invisible tether drawing me closer to him. A pull on my heart that drags me deeper and deeper into the forest, until it leads me to a clearing.

And that's where I see him at last.

"Jonah!" I scream, rushing forward, knowing it could very well be another of the forest's plots.

Still, I run toward my son, where he lies at the base of a tree with bark the color of death. Roots cover him up to the waist, wrapped around his legs and his arms. Collapsing at his side, I find a bed of decaying leaves underneath him, a patch of clover around him. His eyes are closed, and his body is still, but I can see the slightest rise and fall of his chest. I'm not too late.

Something wet lands on his face—tears. My tears. I brush a thumb across his pale face to wipe them away. "I've got you, baby," I whisper.

He doesn't move.

"I'll get you out."

I then pull my knife from my pocket and plunge it into the nearest root.

But it isn't the tree who cries out like I expect it to. It's my son who screams.

I drop the knife and stagger back.

No.

Not him.

All I can see is the knife in his chest. Over and over. By my hand. Him in the grass. Blood. So much blood.

Gods, is this what I'm capable of?

Of course it is, the forest answers.

And I know it's right. Of course it's right. Because I'm the reason Jonah is here. I'm the one who didn't lock the door. I'm the reason he wandered off. Because I didn't care enough. I must have done something wrong, said the wrong thing, forgotten something important. Or maybe I was simply too happy, which led me to let my guard down. Ella made me feel so safe. Jonah brought me life. And the forest is here to take him away.

It's your fault, the forest insists.

And I know it's true. Even if I save him now, it doesn't matter. I don't deserve this happiness. I never did. Happiness is something you earn, and there's no way I've done enough for that. I should have been more careful. Should have listened. Should have tried. Should have watched.

You are the monster, the forest tells me.

And I believe it.

I collapse in on myself, my forehead to my knees. The forest should have me too.

"Do you love him?"

The voice pierces through the fog. Ella. Stern. Gentle. Warm. Determined. I sit up slowly, searching for the source of her voice. But she isn't here.

"Do you love him?" she asks again.

"Yes," I reply, tears streaming like rivulets down my cheeks.

"Would you ever hurt him?"

"I..." I can't finish the sentence. The vision, so clear in my mind, makes it impossible to believe anything. "I love him."

"Your brain lies," Ella says. "You know this. You love him. Would you ever hurt him?"

"No," I whisper. I know it. I want to believe it.

"Would you leave him to die, then?"

I pick up my head and fix my eyes in front of me. On our son, buried beneath the roots of a tree that will claim him forever. And I know I have no other choice. With a deep breath, I drag myself to my feet and reach behind me. I take the bag from my back, and from it, I draw the bat. It glints under some invisible moonlight as I pull it back behind my shoulder.

"Give me back my son!" I scream. I then swing my arms and slam the metal bat against the tree.

Coach always said I had a mean hitting speed.

Bark splinters off the tree, scattering across the forest floor. That same dark red substance oozes out from the fresh wounds, dripping down the sides. But Jonah does not stir. I swing again, more splinters fly. This time, the roots shiver around him, loosening their hold. I drive the bat into the tree once more. An inhuman sound echoes throughout the forest, but I ignore it. The forest will not take him from me.

Another shriek. Panic starts to set in, but I let go of the bat and snatch my knife from the ground. Dropping to Jonah's side once more, I sever the few remaining roots and pull them away.

Jonah's eyes flutter open for just a moment, and I hear him. A soft, unmistakable sigh.

"I've got you," I say again, wiping away the residue left on his skin from the roots. When I unearth him, he appears whole. Alive. I clutch him close to my chest and stand, so aware of how small he is in my arms. Then I clip my flashlight to my jeans with a carabiner and turn to leave.

I take one step before the ground heaves. Crying out, I stagger back, Jonah slipping in my arms. "Jonah, can you hear me?" I ask, but he makes no indication that he does. The earth shifts once more beneath me and knocks me off balance. Jonah and I tumble to the ground and I lose my grip entirely.

Stay, the forest whispers, *and you'll never hurt anyone again.*

But there is a fire in my heart now. I drag myself to my feet. "If you want him," I hiss, "then try to take him."

Writhing roots rise up from the ground and reach towards me, twisting around my ankles. I move quickly and weave out of their path before they can grab me. Too late, I realize that's what the forest wants. I'm even farther from Jonah now, and the roots have already wrapped around his wrists to drag him away.

"You will not have him!" I yell. My shoes pound the ground as I run. Without hesitation, I seize a root holding Jonah's arm and drag my knife across it, and it snaps away with a crunch like breaking bone. For the first time, I see the purple veins in the roots, the color of poison. Of rot. Of sleep.

The forest shrieks when I drive my blade down into another root, thicker this time. The blade comes out soaked in its blood, and the trees hesitate just long enough for me to slip my knife back into my pocket and pick up Jonah, one arm beneath him and one securely around his back.

We're getting out of here, I promise him silently.

There's another scream and the ground shakes once more, but not nearly as strongly as before, and I manage to stay upright. I leave the bat, gripping the flashlight in one hand and clutching Jonah to my chest as I sprint away from the tree, from the forest, from the voices calling me. From empty promises I know will only hold me back.

Stay here.

You'll be safe.

Don't leave.

I'll protect you.

"Lies," I remind myself. The forest may say it can save me, but it will only trap me here forever.

I keep running, weaving around the trees and through the forest, searching for the damaged trunks as my beacons to lead me out. With every step the forest rebels. Branches drop and brush rises to trip me. Screeches and cries echo from the sky above me, the forest's hidden denizens on my trail. But I don't look back. I keep running. All I can think is *Jonah, Jonah, Jonah.*

And after running for what feels like forever, I finally see it. The stone gate. The wooden door. The way out. My feet slam on the ground, and I push myself faster and faster and—

My foot catches. We tumble. I grip Jonah as close to my chest as I can.

And then there is silence as I lie in the grass, breathing, eyes closed, holding my son in my arms as I anticipate the worst.

"Mama?" he asks in a hoarse whisper.

I dare to look, and it's a sky of stars that greets me. Crickets chirping. A gentle breeze and a quiet patter of rain. The ruins in the forest rest safely behind me.

We're on the other side.

We made it.

He stares at me with tired eyes, lids slowly blinking. "Mama?" he asks again. "Is it you?"

"Yes. It's okay now," I whisper back to him, and he buries his head in my chest. "We're going home."

Thirteen Winters

JUSTIN CARLOS ALCALA

"SHE FAVORS OUR FLESH," said Inga's mother. "But will eat well-nigh anything."

Inga's mother never mended from losing Inga and her father thirteen years ago. So, each winter on Inga's birthday, her mother retold the tale. Inga sat at the window nook of their stone cottage, watching the blizzard pass. Her mother tended to Pasulj over the hearth, stirring the white beans and ham hock.

"Livestock, fish, it matters not, as long as its bones are frozen," said Inga's mother. "And she deals cruelties at winter's approach. Chopping of trees, blighting of crops, disease in cattle—anything to nurture desperation come winter. Then, when she deems it, someone always disappears. That's what happened when father took you to find food."

Inga looked out to the wall of evergreens a short distance outside the frosted glass. It once was an ominous sight, a wall that held back chilling terrors. Beyond it, *She* dwelled, waiting to punish anyone bold enough to pass beyond its fronds. Now though, in these confining whiles of the season, these wood-dreaded stories kindled curiosity in such tiresome stretches of cold.

What would it be like to meet her again, Inga wondered. *Would she recognize me now that I've grown?*

"Except you returned, my plum," said Inga's mother as if reading her mind. "Call her what you wish. Ice Hag, Winter's Handmaiden, Grandmother Snow—she returned you to me, a little baby left in a tree. I only wish my prayers were loud enough for God to return your father, too."

Inga's mother set two wooden bowls on their crooked table, then used a rag to lift the cauldron from the fire before pouring dinner.

"Make a wish, my plum," said Inga's mother. "To another year survived."

Inga ran to her seat, anticipating the special yearly Pasulj her mother made. She put her face to the bowl, inhaling the stew's breath. The thirteen-year-old grew hungrier these days, and a diminished harvest didn't help. She made a wish, then downed her supper absentminded of any decorum. By the time she'd slurped the last from her bowl, she found her mother sitting in wait, a paper package twined in string atop the table.

"Happy birthday, my plum," said Inga's mother.

"Oh mother, you didn't have to," said Inga.

Her mother crafted a gift for Inga each year, but this was different. The packaging and string meant she'd purchased it, a rarity for a woodcutter family. Inga stretched over the table and received her present, clawing the tissue like a wild beast. With the package strewn open, Inga crooned. She held up the blue cloak, its hood laced with rabbit fur.

"Oh, mother, it's beautiful," said Inga.

"It's not every day a girl comes of age," said Inga's mother.

Inga twirled the cloak over her shoulders and danced to unheard music. She took to her own reflection in the window before rushing to her mother and embracing her.

"This is the best birthday ever," said Inga. "I've never felt so lively."

"If only you could show it to Anežka, she'd fiddle you a birthday song," Inga's mother lamented, genuflecting towards the fireplace cross.

Inga thought back to her dinnertime wish. She and Anežka were neighbors of the woods, living six hills and a ravine apart. Anežka schooled in the village and brought back with her the loveliest books borrowed from her pedagogue. She always shared the stories with her forest sister, teaching Inga to read during sleepovers and river picnics. The two had been inseparable for nearly a decade until the hag claimed her last year. Unlike Inga's father, who Inga lost before she could remember, Anežka's loss cut deep. Without her, everything was tedious. Without her, nothing kept the meaning it once held.

"Poor child. One year ago today," said Inga's mother.

"Maybe she's still out there," said Inga. "Surviving."

"Oh, my plum, don't listen to me. I've matured like a cemetery, bleaker, and wider."

Inga sniggered.

"Come," Inga's mother smiled. "Let us celebrate and repair this blackened mood."

For the rest of the evening, Inga and her mother rejoiced with pudding, pie, and a cup of cheer. By middle-night, Inga's mother slept so deep, and snored so loud, not even the roof caving in would wake her. But not Inga. She lay on the opposite side of their bed, staring out as the snowstorm calmed with thoughts of Anežka. The winds hushed and snow ceased as if commanded by unknown forces. The white canopy mirrored moonlight, producing a cobalt glow.

Inga crept out of bed, looking into the woods. To her surprise, a glimmer like candlelight shimmered a great distance away. Inga squinted, noticing a swell in the flame as if someone fed it. She tiptoed to her clothes-trunk, hurried on her boots, then wrapped herself in her new cloak. With the quietest tug she could muster, Inga unlatched and opened the door, entering nighttime's haven. Snow crushed beneath her feet as she navigated to the timberline, eyes fixed on the light.

There was a fire where no home should be. Life existed where it had been forbidden.

Although her mother had banned Inga from entering during the cold months, she knew these woods well. She navigated through Snake's Pass, closing the distance between herself and the mysterious flame. There was no fear, though her once-full belly gurgled with a strange appetite. Inga felt revitalized to be in the wildernesses again, her blood surging with anticipation. A stride led to a yard, which turned to a mile. By the time she'd crossed the frozen stream, Inga knew what lured her in these woods. She'd met it all before.

A fiddler whose music sounded like hello and ended in goodbye played along a bonfire. Within its backdrop, a thatch-roofed hut with a cinder-spewing chimney sat secured by a door of bones. A tall man, bearded like a saint and blackened with frostbite, mumbled as he shambled around the dwelling. Inga lingered beside the last oak of the woods, inspecting the fireside musician.

An auburn-haired girl in rags strummed a violin, besmirched in dirt and bruises. Her lips were slit in several places, marked by scabs. A chain enveloped her ankle, staked into a rock of ice, and a kitchen cleaver with a collection of chicken heads lay at her side.

"Anežka," Inga said, emerging through the wood line.

Anežka claimed the cleaver, leaping to her feet. Inga closed the distance, arms stretched out for an embrace. Anežka's eyes grew wide, and her jaw clenched. She looked at the man circling the cottage. The man refused to quit his ceaseless circle. Anežka's eyes returned to Inga.

"It's me, *Inga,*" said Inga. "I'm so glad you're alive, my friend. I saw your light from home."

Anežka's mouth drew into an O. Where teeth should be now grinned only jagged glass. The wounds within her gums bled, unbearable to look at. Inga winced, but refused to release her gaze.

"By God's grace," said Inga. "What has She done to you?"

Anežka's jaw moved to speak but only let out a groan. She sank her head, overcome.

"Anežka, I wished for this," said Inga. She donned a counterfeit smile meant to disarm tension. "It's my birthday today, and I asked for this very instance. Come, I'll free you."

Anežka face drew blank. As if bucked by a mule, her body bounded to life. Anežka raised the cleaver, and with a screech, charged at Inga.

"Wait, Anežka, no," said Inga.

Inga grabbed at Anežka's wrists. Anežka was taller and stronger than Inga in years past, but now hunger and neglect had worn her down. Inga clutched the cleaver midair, stopping its route. Beaten, but not conquered, Anežka drove her shoulder into Inga's chest, and the pair fell to the snow. Anežka used her leverage to mount atop Inga, raising the hatchet once more. But Inga bucked her hips, tossing Anežka off her.

"Stop this, I beg of you," said Inga. "She'll hear us."

Inga crawled backwards, Anežka slinking in pursuit. The chain ran taut as Anežka chased her prey, jerking the girl backwards. Growling,

Anežka upstretched the hatchet as though to throw it. Inga shielded her face.

"Please, Anežka, don't," said Inga. "You're mad from hunger."

Anežka didn't take the time to consider. She hurled the blade at Inga. The cleaver spun mid-flight. Only its handle struck Inga, sending a web of agony through her ribs. Infuriated by the torment, Inga reactively picked up the blade. She aimed the knife at Anežka's shoulder, hoping a wound would knock sense into her old friend. But the knife missed its mark a second time, electing blood where it once chose warning. The sharp part of the blade plunged into Anežka's heart. Anežka fell rearward into the snow, hand pointed at the bone door. Inga rushed and huddled over her best friend.

"Oh, no," said Inga. "Not like this. This is not what I wished for."

Anežka's body twitched. She dropped her pointing hand, and her eyes went dull. Anežka took one last desperate gurgle before going still. Inga rested her head on her friend and wept. She didn't know how long she sat crying, but the shock seemed to keep Inga warm. It also inspired an anger in her she couldn't tame.

The dead man's mumbling reminded Inga there was a task at hand. Inga collected the grisly hatchet, plucking it from its sinewy sheath, and approached the cottage. To her chagrin, the bone door now stood agape. She waited for the raptly frostbitten man to circle the back of the hut and then, with impetus, Inga entered.

Inside, a hearth crackled, accompanied by an uninterested cat. Inga could see the shambling man's silhouette passing along the grimy windows. Roots from an invisible tree hung from the ceiling, and a round table chalked in stars preserved a book in its center. Inga recognized the hardcover as a storybook Anežka loaned her many times throughout their childhood. With no sign of the hag, Inga hurried to the tome, flipping its dog-eared pages. The short stories were as Inga remembered except for one. Marked with a quill were notes beneath the tale of the Crookwhistle Coven. Inga read through the tale. The last line described how the brave woodsman slew the trio of witches before claiming their beautiful prisoner as his bride, but it was marked with an annotation in Anežka's handwriting.

~~THE END~~

But it was not the end. For Snežana endured, swearing vengeance on those who slew her sisters. Once healed, she hunted her foes and arranged conditions to starve them. When the brave woodsman grew foolish enough to take his new daughter out to unearth root-foods, Snežana struck. She hexed the woodsman and devoured the baby unseasoned. For when a hag eats an infant, she births a hag-spawn in a week-and-a-day. She gives the ordinary child to mortals to rear until its thirteenth birthday, when the hag reclaims it to replace her coven sisters.

Inga dropped her knife, searching the room for reasoning. Where the cat once stood, now a wrinkled crone, gaunt with pallid skin and crowned in pale hair, stared. She wore a tattered frock and gripped a doll made of twigs. Inga's breathing quickened, and her breath drew icy. Yet she suffered no chill in the air. The hag raised the doll, offering it to her. Inga stretched to take it, noticing her now waxy blue skin. Inga took in her hands, clawed with talons. A loud burble from her stomach drew in a hunger that had been growing in her for days.

The hag stared at Inga's belly as her stomach moaned. She pointed to the man's shadow circling the hut. Inga couldn't explain why cold skin and frozen bones made her famished. She only knew that a hunger grew inside her, one that yet felt unsatisfied. For thirteen years, that meal outside had conditioned itself in wait for Inga's homecoming. For thirteen years, the Ice Hag had nurtured that reprisal, waiting for her daughter's advent. For vengeance is best served cold, and in the opinion of ice hags... so is supper.

The Door in Her Throat

FENDY S. TULODO

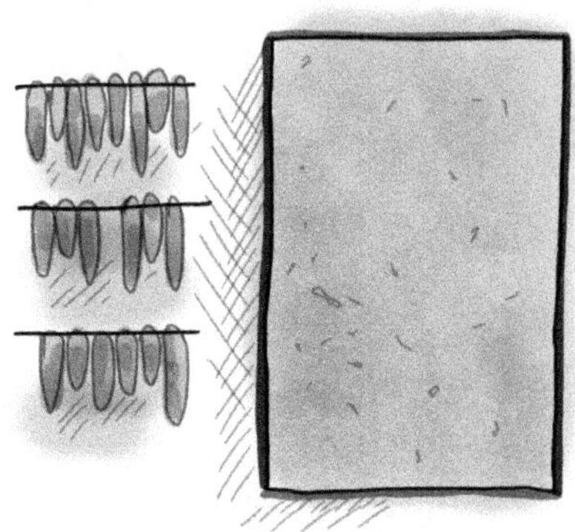

LIME DUST COATED HALF of it behind the fish-drying racks, this first discovery. A dying fridge's hum came from the warm, vibrating rectangle—no handle, no hinges, just rusted iron bolted stubborn into stone. That faint pulse? Only just noticed—like it breathed. No one else heard the sound. Not even Afina's mother. Not even when Afina pressed her ear to the surface and whispered, "Do you hear it? It's... calling."

Afina was sixteen when the door first opened. Not literally, not in the obvious way. There was no dramatic creaking or glowing outline. It happened in the middle of a conversation, a small argument over dried squid and the family's reputation. Her mother's voice cracked in a place it never had before, and Afina saw something: a tiny shift behind her mother's eyes, like a rusted lock loosening.

"What did you say?" her mother asked.

"I said I'm not going to marry him," Afina replied. "I said it ten times already."

"You think you're better than your sisters now? Is that it? You—little thing—you think because you read a few books you get to throw your life in the canal?"

Afina didn't answer. Her hand was still on the iron rectangle. The heat in her palm was spreading up her wrist. The humming was louder now. Inside her chest.

Her mother slapped the fish table hard. "Get back to the stall! Before I rip those books out of your ears!"

That's when Afina saw it: a flickering shape in the center of the iron door, right where her hand had been. Like a window had opened just long enough to show her another *her*, standing in another market, with clean fingers and soft eyes and no blood underneath her nails.

And then it was gone.

She didn't tell anyone. Not even Jero. Until it happened once more.

Jero was the only one who ever listened. That extra year made him taller, darker from the sun, shoulders peeling. Anger never raised his voice. Whittling boats from driftwood was his harbor habit. Kids would buy them, though never sea-worthy. Tourists loved his wave paintings most—brush strokes that almost looked like real ocean, if you squinted just right.

"I saw something again," Afina whispered.

"When?"

"This morning."

"The door again?"

She nodded. Her fingers were wrapped in gauze from helping her father gut something too big for her grip.

"What was it this time?"

"Me. But not me."

Jero didn't laugh. He never laughed at things like that. He just handed her a half-carved boat and said, "Show me where."

The door behind the fish racks wasn't humming anymore. It was cold and heavy again, like it had never moved. Jero tapped it with a coin. Nothing. Tapped again. Nothing.

"It's dead," he said.

"It was breathing yesterday," Afina replied. "I swear."

Jero tilted his head, eyes narrowing. "Maybe it only breathes for you."

Afina didn't know whether to be afraid or proud. Both, maybe.

That night, the door came back in her dream. But this time, it wasn't iron. It was bone. And it opened into her own mouth.

She woke up coughing.

The third time it opened, it was real. Not a dream. Not a shimmer. Real.

It happened on the morning she turned down the matchmaker again. Her father's face was stone. Her mother's hands were trembling, but not from anger. This time, Afina saw it clearly—her mother was scared. Not of her, but of something else. Maybe of what they would say. Maybe of what it would mean to lose a daughter to thinking.

"You will go," her father said, not asking.

"I won't."

"You will go!" he shouted, stabbing his spoon into his rice so hard it cracked the bowl.

Afina stood.

And the humming began again.

Stronger.

Not behind the fish rack.

But in her own body.

She ran.

Ran until her knees burned and her braid came undone.

The iron door was waiting. Same shape. Same size. But it was no longer bolted to the wall.

It was standing on its own.

Open.

Inside, there was nothing but fog. And a smell like old wind.

"Afina?" Jero's voice came from behind.

She turned, breath wild. "It opened."

"I see it."

"I can go."

"Go where?"

She stepped forward. "Anywhere that isn't here."

Jero caught her wrist. His fingers were warm, familiar. "Then let me come."

She didn't pull away. But she didn't move either. "You'll hate it. I know you will. You'll try to fix it. And this place... this version of me... it doesn't need fixing."

"What if I love it?" he asked.

Afina laughed once. Sharp. Almost bitter. "What I feel for you? You can't even imagine."

He blinked. "What?"

She stepped into the fog before he could answer.

The new world was too quiet.

No boats. No gulls. No market yelling. Just trees. Thin ones. Their arms stretched too far, grasping at nothing. Underfoot, the ground felt strange—not moss-soft, but tangled like loose yarn before spinning.

Three steps in, Afina froze. Something wasn't right.

Her voice.

She tried to call. Nothing came.

Not air. Not a scratch. Not even vibration.

Her throat was a locked cage.

She sat under one of the stretch-trees and cried. Ugly, hot tears. They came with no sound. Only the shake of her shoulders.

When the first figure appeared, she wasn't surprised. It looked like her—taller, with clean hair and calm eyes.

It didn't speak. Just nodded once, then placed a hand on Afina's chest.

The humming came back. Inside her ribs. Then—

The sound rushed out.

A sob.

A scream.

A name: "Jero!"

But there was no one to hear it.

Only the fog.

Only the her that wasn't her.

Back in the market, Jero sat alone by the door. The iron had fallen. Cracked. Cold again.

He waited six days.

Each night, he slept beside the frame. Left food. Spoke stories to the silence.

On the seventh day, he carved a boat bigger than any before. Left it standing upright by the iron.

He whispered, "If you find this... know I believed you. I still do."

Then he walked away.

He didn't hear the door hum behind him.

And he didn't see the boat float sideways into the fog.

Time blurred together for Afina. That pale glow overhead never shifted—no sunrise, no sunset. Strange how the bread kept appearing by her sleeping spot, how the broth stayed warm in chipped mugs, though nobody brought it. Flavorless, yet unlike anything she knew. Her muscles forgot how to ache. Her feet never blistered, even though she walked every hour she was awake.

But the other-her kept appearing. Always watching. Always quiet.

Afina hated her.

That unblinking stare of hers bothered Afina most. The shine of her skin felt like disappointment, strange—but distant. And that smile—plump and gentle, as if no one had ever told her "No" sharp enough to crack it.

"Say something!" Afina finally yelled. "Just say something, you... fake thing!"

The other-her tilted her head. Then walked away.

Afina threw the empty mug at the tree. It didn't even break.

She wanted to scream again, but the fog swallowed the sound, like it didn't matter here.

Maybe it didn't.

One morning, the ground opened up.

Not with a crack or a collapse. It folded. Like paper. A neat triangle just under Afina's feet, revealing stairs made of the same pale material as the trees.

She stood there a long time before climbing down.

The air was warm. Not humid, but soft. Kind. Like something that understood her more than people ever did.

At the bottom, there was a room. Walls glowed. No roof. Just four corners trapping a long table. On it: a knife, a mirror, and a notebook.

She touched the mirror first.

Her face looked the same. But her eyes didn't. The girl in the mirror looked exhausted. Not from running, but from feeling too much for too long. From giving away love like sugar cubes in a flood.

She reached for the notebook next. It was blank.

Except on the last page.

In small, scribbled letters, it said:

"You will lose everything if you wait for them to see it."

She almost dropped it.

Then she picked up the knife.

And suddenly, she was back at the market.

The noise hit her like a slap. Frying oil. Voices. Bargaining. A kid screaming about peanuts. Afina spun around in the crowd. No fog. No stretch-trees. The air was thick and familiar. Spiced. Loud.

She ran to the fish racks.

The iron door was there.

Broken.

And beside it stood her mother.

Afina froze.

Her mother looked thinner. A little more tired. But her eyes didn't change.

"You came back," she said, not smiling.

Afina didn't answer.

"What now?" her mother asked. "You expect me to hug you after what you did?"

"I don't expect anything," Afina replied.

"You think running away proves you're special? That your pain's deeper than ours?"

"No," Afina said. "But it's mine. And I'm allowed to live with it."

Her mother stepped forward, hands tight. "We suffered too, you know! We bled too! You think you invented sadness?"

Afina almost laughed. "I think I learned it from you."

She found Jero two streets away.

He was selling boats again. Smaller this time. Not painted.

He saw her and dropped one mid-carve.

"Afina?"

"I thought you wouldn't be here."

"I never left."

She walked to the edge of his booth. "I didn't think you'd wait."

"I didn't know how."

He looked at her face. Then her hands. Then her eyes.

"You're not the same," he said.

"I didn't try to be."

He nodded slowly. "I want to ask what happened... but I think I shouldn't."

"Good."

They didn't hug. Not yet.

But Afina reached out and touched the edge of the table. Just close enough for her fingers to brush against his.

Jero didn't move.

So she stepped back.

"I'm not here to stay," she said.

His lips parted. "What?"

"There's another door. A better one."

"Then why did you come back?"

"To say thank you."

He swallowed. "For what?"

"For loving me... just enough."

"Enough for what?"

"To let me go."

The second door was inside the cracked iron one. She'd never seen it, not till now. It glowed soft, a pale ring, like light caught under thin cloth. Afina opened it with her fingers. No humming this time, only silence. She stepped in.

And this time, the fog didn't greet her. Instead, there was a long table and three versions of her sitting across from each other. One wore a wedding dress stained with fish blood. One held a baby who didn't cry. And the last one had no mouth.

Afina sat down. "I know what this means," she said. No one answered. "I can't rescue you," she murmured. "And I can't become you." Still nothing. "But I can walk away."

That's when they all stood. All three. And behind them, a final door opened—a shape carved into light.

Afina stepped toward it. Not fast. Not trembling. She turned her head once. No one followed.

And that was okay.

Because some doors... some doors you walk through alone.

The final door didn't lead to a world. Not the way the others had. There were no trees. No sky. No echo of the market, no fog.

It led to a space made of breath.

Like the inside of a lung that belonged to something ancient.

Afina stepped forward and the ground formed under her. Each step created a path. Each breath shaped the air. Here, everything responded to her—not her wishes, not her thoughts, but her *truths*. The ugly ones. The ones she'd shoved down until they rang inside her ribs.

She opened her mouth and spoke her name. Not just *"Afina."* But the name she whispered when she hated herself. The name she almost gave up when she thought being obedient was the only way to be loved.

She said it aloud.

And the space didn't collapse.

It held her.

A shape grew in the distance.

Not a person.

Not a mirror.

Not a door.

But a chair.

Wooden. Familiar. The one from the house her father built with his hands when she was a child. That chair remembered her gentle hands working through tangles, never tugging. No thanks came, just her mother's constant humming—that same sad-song melody, like someone had stitched grief into musical notes long ago.

Afina sat.

The chair didn't break.

She wept again. Not from sadness. But from the way the air let her be.

It didn't ask her to explain. Didn't tell her she was too much, or too loud, or too distant.

For the first time, she wasn't escaping.

She was *arriving*.

Then the door spoke.

Not in words.

In feeling.

A pulse ran through the space, gentle and slow. Not a heartbeat. A *recognition*.

She closed her eyes.

A new door formed behind her eyelids.

This one didn't open outward.

It opened inward.

Into a memory she had locked away.

She was twelve again.

Hiding under the stairs while her parents argued.

Her father shouting about dignity. Her mother screaming about the shame Afina brought by speaking out in school. Her voice had been too loud. Her question too bold.

"She asks *why,*" her mother snapped, "as if we have time for that!"

"She thinks life's about choices," her father growled. "Who taught her that?"

Knees pulled tight against her ribs, Afina bit back tears. Even crying felt dangerous now—too loud, too messy, too much.

That was the moment the first door started growing inside her.

She didn't know it yet.

But it had lived in her throat ever since.

Back in the chair, Afina inhaled.

Long.

Deep.

And when she exhaled, the air around her *cracked*.

A new path opened. No invitation. No signs.

But she understood.

It was time to leave.

Not because she was being pushed out.

But because she was ready.

She stood.

No hesitation.

And the chair—like everything else here—disappeared behind her.

Not gone.

Just released.

She stepped back into the world at dusk.

The market lights were flickering on. She heard laughing. Haggling. Someone burned corn. The smell punched her in the chest. Real. Unmistakable. And full of memory.

Afina didn't return to the fish stall.

She walked to the small alley behind the harbor wall. Where the door had first appeared. Where she'd first heard the hum.

It was gone.

But the ground still held its shape.

Jero was sitting there.

Back leaned against the wall.

Same quiet eyes.

But different too. Like he'd grown heavier inside, not in a bad way, but in a real way.

"You look different," he said.

"I'm not."

He tilted his head. "Liar."

She smiled. "Okay. Maybe I am."

He looked up. "Did you find what you were looking for?"

She sat beside him. Close. Not touching.

"I didn't find anything," she said.

"Then what?"

"I stopped looking."

He didn't say anything for a while. The night settled around them.

Then he said, "That sounds... painful."

"It is."

"Would you go back?"

"No."

"Would you want me to come?"

Afina shook her head. "It's not that kind of place."

"Then what kind is it?"

Chin propped on folded knees, she studied the room.

"Some places... they shrink your wants just by existing. And be okay with that."

They didn't get married.

They didn't run away.

They didn't fight for anything noble or poetic or unforgettable.

They grew apart. Quietly. Kindly. In their own time.

And Afina never spoke of the door again.

Except once.

To a girl with her same eyes, years later, who screamed too loudly at dinner one night and stormed off because her drawing had been thrown away.

Afina followed her out and found her sitting on the steps with her little fists clenched. She sat close, said nothing at first, then asked, "Want to see where doors begin?"

The girl turned, staring. "Like, real ones?"

Afina smiled. "Something better."

That night, she told the girl about a fog, about a place where chairs remember your mother's tune, about love that doesn't wait, about versions of yourself who wear different endings, and about a space that listens when you stop screaming.

"Was it scary?" the girl asked.

"Yeah," Afina whispered.

"Did it hurt?"

Afina thought about Jero, about her mother's trembling hand, about that final chair. "Yeah," she said. "It hurt more than anything."

The girl leaned her head on Afina's shoulder and said nothing else.

Because some stories don't need to be understood right away.

Some stories are doors. Waiting to be opened.

The Library of the Lost

RUKMAN RAGAS

ON BOMBED SHORES OF war-torn countries, buildings belonging to the Covenant of Greater Buildings of Lost, Hurt, and Other Complications were sorely needed. However, Marianne, the resident Museum of Hurt, was convinced that my skills were better served elsewhere.

"You should find a better place," she declared flatly.

I scoffed at the implication. A better place. What Marianne meant was that I should find a *different* place.

"Why don't you say what you really mean?" I asked. I could feel her ire, the pillars of her handsome brownwood gleaming in the fading light.

"Well, Ari, you could be anywhere. Stop chaining yourself here. You have no one."

I huffed, "Dear Mari" —she *hated* being called that— "are you calling yourself no one?"

She wasn't wrong. Marianne seldom was, but she was also not the sort to mince words. We were neighboring buildings of the Covenant of Greater Buildings, but while she was the only wooden structure in the slums, a Museum of Hurt, I was a burnt ruin of a library rumored to host the blood sucking ratha kateris rather than books.

"You haven't had a patron in the last twenty years."

Ah, there it was.

"And look at you, covered in soot and dirt and paint. You served your term. Now it's time to leave this place and move on," she chided, like a pecking mother hen.

"But if I leave, who will keep you company?" I deflected.

The old building grumbled, clearly not pleased.

"I can't go anywhere else, Marianne. I'm a burnt library of an exiled people. If I go anywhere else, I will no longer be Ari. I am not you," I finally managed to say, before finding the ground more interesting than it rightfully was.

Buildings could sulk, and while I had none of the subtlety or windows needed for it, Marianne was a master. Her windows promptly clanged shut and the several feet of air between us still managed to feel sullen.

"If you are going to stay here, then you will have to do what you are meant to do," she finally said.

I was saved from answering when the evening's monsoon struck our city, its winds forcing us to shutter ourselves to protect our patrons—Marianne at least. I haven't had a patron since my burning.

I didn't know that was about to change.

⚷

That night, when the moon cleared the horizon and crested the sky, a young man, drunk and wet, never knowing nor caring where he went, crashed into my single corrugated gate. He fell inside my compound, collapsing in an unseemly heap.

It was surprising that he'd managed to find me. He must have been lost enough. I did my usual theatrics, shaking my corrugated iron sheets and sending a haunting breeze through the courtyard.

The young man was too tired to care. He cursed, then sighed as his legs failed him in his attempt to get back up. He didn't look like someone who had somewhere to be or anywhere to go, brows furrowed and eyes pensive, the same expression so many of my patrons had at the beginning. I wondered who had sent this audacious creature, and then I looked across the street at Marianne. She was shuttered, but I could feel the smugness radiating off her yellow lanterns' glow.

I knew better than to ask her to take him back. Marianne's for the hurt and bleeding, and the city, with its constant war and inconsistent aid, was filled to the brim with those. She could barely handle the wounded, her tiled floors quickly stained with blood because there's only so much of it you can wipe away without leaving a mark. No, this one wasn't hurt in a way for Marianne to justify taking him in.

So, with a long sigh, my doors manifested around him and opened, accounting for his tired eyes. Marianne's wind chimes were the only sign of her amusement. It had been years since I deemed someone lost enough to shelter. That's the thing about war. With your life in danger, you always must run. Survival became the purpose, became your way and you didn't have the luxury of being lost.

However, the war had ended months ago, just enough time for people to realize all the things that had been wrenched away from them, long enough to learn that they have no way left to find. And I wasn't the most appealing choice for the lost, if I was being honest. A structure barely standing, blackened walls almost fully open to the sky? Symbol of the burning that started it all. All I hosted were burnt books and bad memories, and I had no intent to welcome tired souls.

I turned away from Marianne apologetically, lighting up my broken windows, their pale yellow glow becoming false signage. I couldn't be lax in my duties. The old hag would report me if I tried to coast along. The first of the lost had found me.

The lost were everywhere. You could find one wandering your workplace, coming and going, every day the same. Then, one day, when the job fires her, she would be that. Lost. Or you may have even heard it in your drunken neighbor's voice, singing a loud love song, mourning a love lost. A student on the steps before the grand courts, not knowing why she was so...lost.

They were everywhere, and wherever they were, we the Libraries followed. Most lost found their path soon. I've seen them stumble, I've seen them fall, but they felt for the waystones or chased that pinprick of light. For the lucky few, there was rope thrown, and they hung on to it so tightly. And somehow, they found their way out.

But not everyone had a light during their dark nights. And not everyone knew where the waystones were. They remained lost and the Libraries took them in. We didn't find them their way; that would be preposterous. To each is their own path. No, we were waystops, places they could rest despite being lost. If they found their way, we sent them off with a celebration to haunt the halls of the undead. And if they didn't, that was fine too. They stayed with us, amidst all the things that once had a home.

This young man was a lost thing indeed. His suit had seen better times and the scent of beer was heavy on his breath. I hurried him inside, my windows snapping. I wasn't the library of New York, where sprawling tomes sheltered tales within pages; nor was I the Library of Rio, with a verdant pasture of languages and warmth. No, I was the burnt library of a city abandoned. I had no tomes to comfort him, no languages to fill his ears. I had only an ember of warmth from my burning and I gave it to him.

Guiding him to my ever-burning bonfire, I found an old potato box. It'd been a while since I'd had guests. Deciding it would do, I slid the box into place beside the shivering man, the dust stirring on a floor that hadn't seen movement for months. He sat and stared into the fire. He wasn't very bright, I decided. It didn't bother me because whatever the rumors said, we weren't only open to the erudite and the learners. We Libraries were safe havens, first and foremost, and even a burnt one like me knew that.

He didn't question the building that formed doors wherever it liked or possessed an interior larger than it had the right to be. He didn't think of the olai leaves strewn around nor the paperbacks around the open flame. And above all, he didn't question me taking form in front of him—what little form I had left to take. My burning had stripped away most of my physical essence, and what remained let me form something that left much to be desired. My face was a patchwork of whatever phantom flesh I could piece together. A void stretched where my left eye used to be and my right cheek was completely burnt away, revealing the bright white teeth and bloody pages beneath.

He didn't flinch, didn't notice nor give any indication that he registered my presence.

I was relieved but also disappointed. The horror I inspired grew tiresome, but there was such sharp giddiness in being seen clearly, in watching their faces turn white with fear, then mellow with pity. I wanted to be seen as not as the burnt, defunct library. I wanted to be seen with pity or fear, both a testament to my suffering. Hadn't I earned that much at least?

"Who are you?" he asked, finally looking up from warming his hands. The fire's light threw his battered features into sharp contrast. His nose was bulbous and hooked, his face dark and just a little too horse-like to be called handsome.

"Does it matter?" I replied. "I'm someone who gives sanctuary."

"No," he said, teeth chattering. "You *are* a sanctuary."

"That too." I took a paperback lying on the ground and slowly fed it to the fire, page by page. It was a classic and I could already hear the mob screaming about the book burning. Another had already burnt me though and I couldn't care less.

He hunched closer to the flames, warming his palms.

This was the second uncomfortable silence I'd had to sit through in a day and this one was punctuated by our unfamiliarity, while the conversation with Marianne was because we had known each other for too long.

"How long can I stay?" he asked me suddenly.

"As you said, I'm a sanctuary. Stay as long as you need, as long as you don't have a way."

"What should I do in return?"

"I don't run a bed and breakfast to trade in exchanges. You don't have to do anything."

His lips pursed together, and he lifted his head. It bothered him, this one-sided transaction. "I insist," he said. "There's no free lunch, Library. I would rather not be indebted to you."

I wanted to laugh. But my spectral body wasn't capable of doing it; even the voice I projected was a manipulation of the air that flowed through my halls. I made sure to look at him, up and down, at his tattered suit, the cracked pair of glasses held together by cello tape and prayers, the spindly body beneath. A library had to find some way to convey its condescension.

"Let's say I do it your way," I said after a while, just long enough to make him fidget. "What can you offer me in return? What do you have left, stranger?"

At that, he fell quiet. The ones who have something left—well, they can't find me. I'm the library of the hopeless lost, aren't I? (The Commission of Greater Libraries had asked me to be more 'nurturing' and less 'snarky' but I found the hopeless preferred some honest snark over a veneer of pity. They had enough of it themselves and didn't need me to add to their supply.)

I spoke again, softer this time, for I knew the hurt of having nothing is better than having the facts thrown at your face. "Take what I give you and take it without shame. I don't give you space out of benevolence. I was made to be a sanctuary. *Your* sanctuary. It is my duty and my purpose to offer space for the hopeless lost."

He didn't ask again. I left without a word, fading away into the walls, my soul stretched thin and my inkheart barely beating. That was one of the last paperbacks I had just burnt, and I felt my form lose some of its substance. Ah, I would make do. The burnt library was only half alive anyway.

I didn't think of the lost man I housed for the next few days, even when I spread dead leaves and cobbled webs around my eaves. For atmosphere. Definitely not to discourage any other potential guests; what makes you think that? I am a good, responsible library. Not thinking is a skill I've perfected, so I rested back into my form, not thinking and hibernating.

But the next day I woke up, my eaves were clean and my walls washed. The floor had been mopped enough that I could see my reflection on it if I were to take my corporeal form, and the fresh coat of white paint was sticky on my outer walls.

The culprit was busy making a sign. His brow was creased with concentration and his newly acquired dress, one a maiden I'd housed in my early days left after she gave birth, was already paint streaked.

I manifested before him, without the slightest effort to hide my grotesque countenance.

"What do you think you are doing?" I asked him sternly. Or tried asking sternly.

He fell back, laughing. That wasn't the response I expected for my fury.

"S-sorry," he snorted out, with tears in his eyes. "Just that I didn't expect the paint to make such a difference." He broke into another fit of giggles and I finally took a long look at myself.

My ethereal form had not escaped his treatment of my actual walls. The skin, which used to inspire fear in its soot-covered state, now was covered in snowy white paint, and clothing had been stripped away to reveal nothing beneath. By that, I meant literally nothing, as I don't bother to manifest other body parts when I have my long robe of dirt to cover me. I quickly brought my arms to cover the air where my torso should have been. I looked like one of those theater puppets and I almost screamed. Hundred years of cultivating a refined image, and all it took was one drunk brat who couldn't sleep for a night to ruin it.

"What in the seven hells do you think you are doing?" I repeated.

"As you said, earning my keep." He seemed awfully, almost sinisterly, excited at the prospect. "You are one dirty library, after all."

"Did it ever occur to you that maybe, *just maybe,* there was a reason for the dirt and ruin? A library of the lost cannot look like a mansion for the living, after all."

He didn't even look up from his sign. "Don't kid yourself. No one in their right mind would mistake you for a mansion."

"Anyway, the point is that you have to stop this at once." I lifted my nose up, trying to mimic Marianne's authority.

"The point is, I won't be stopping. You invited me to stay as long as I need to, Library. I am not living in this—"he gestured flamboyantly at the general surroundings— "dump of a place."

To say I was offended was an understatement. But incapable of doing more than huff and puff, as I had offered sanctuary first, I disappeared.

The next day, I discovered new flapping pages on my cloak. When I made my way toward the bookchambers, I found my unwelcome patron had brought in a new shelf.

Dear reader, I almost screeched in response because it was full of Joyce Carol Oates. Now, I'm not a judgy type—a library cannot afford to be—but when I had dark corners to be populated, I knew just whose books to use.

"What is this?" I asked him.

"A library, by definition, needs books, and I found them in an abandoned home." That's all he said even as I screeched at him for his lack of taste.

He went about shelving the books as if he couldn't hear me.

"The newest patron you've sent is frighteningly annoying, Marianne," I said as I perched on her eaves. She hated it when I did that. Said it reminded her of the pigeons. Good.

"Finally, you get to experience what I feel with you." The old building was laughing, clearly amused enough to disregard a ghostly remnant's perch. She also seemed to find my white coat of paint extremely funny.

"I want him gone," I said. "You could have kept him."

"You are a library of the lost, Ari, just as I am the Museum of the Hurt. Just as I cannot let the hurt leave me hurting and with no salve for their wounds, you cannot abandon the lost. His wounds of the body are healed, but as for his wounds of the heart, that's another matter," she replied quite sternly. "Hosting a guest is good for you after being decrepit for years."

"You could have sent him to Collosso. He is also a library, is he not?" I whined, unwilling to let my case go this easily.

"Yes, and Collosso is a library who takes his duties very seriously. He deserves some rest, unlike another library of my acquaintance. He even provided some books to your patron." It was clear she wouldn't be moved that easily.

I sulked on my way back, making sure Marianne could clearly see me dragging my old robe somberly across the distance between her towering building and my burnt shack. I didn't usually walk but I'd found that the method of movement was quite conducive to expressing unwillingness.

I was not willing to accept defeat. Hosting a patron was one thing, but not this one. He irked me in ways I couldn't articulate.

It looked like I might have to break one of the library tenets. I was going to find this lost man his path.

Now, wayfinding was not really my expertise, even when I hosted rebels back in my heyday. But even the most juvenile knew the way to the future was often stuck in the past.

So, chirpy as a songbird, I wrested the information from Colloso, the big brute. He wasn't particularly happy about it, but it's not like what I asked for was illegal. The Commission expected its libraries to be well-versed in their patrons, after all. Armed with the knowledge, I visited my messy meddler's part of the town.

There, rearing up lonesome, was a memorial.

Memorials were never really good news. They were pale shadows of what was once there. Memorials in a war-torn land, in particular, were hurtful renditions of lives that couldn't be protected, of homes lost to the senseless machine that demanded blood, again and again. The grander they were, the worse the massacre, for the survivors tried to assuage their guilt by spending as much as they could to prove they cared.

And this memorial was beautiful. A carved maiden stood on a pavilion, holding onto a lamp with diagonal pillars sticking out from her feet. On her stone face were tear trails and when I moved closer, I realized the shapes at her base weren't pillars. They were stone hands rising from a mound of concrete bodies. The whole base was covered with tens of thousands of names. They were imperfect and asymmetric, but I could feel the pain radiating off them.

A library keeps records and I keep lost records: of the lost and what's owed to them. I traced my fingers over the etched names, searching for their pain, so someone would know their stories. Someone should carry it on. It's only right that the lost are remembered too.

We huddle beneath the tarps emblazoned with the red cross. They said they won't bomb.

But the sky keeps raining fire.

My fingers found another.

Amma... amma... I'm scared. It's so loud. So loud. I'M SCARED AMMA.

A thousand stories like that. Ten thousand left unsaid.

A library couldn't cry. We didn't have the form for it after all and tears are so uniquely human. But without tears or sound, I wept that day. I wept for the razed past and the barren future and the man who had nothing to go back to, no past to ground his future. I wept as only libraries could for their patrons.

When I went back, he was waiting for me. He'd never told me his name, I realized. From the books in his hand, he must have visited Colloso again.

"So, Library, now you know."

"Now I know." I manifested a phantasmagoric vision in front of him, making sure my robe was tight around me this time.

"Do you pity me?" he asked, in that weary tone of someone who had seen enough pity to last a lifetime.

"Do I look like I'm in a state to pity anyone?" I questioned back, waving at my decrepit halls. His paint only covered a wall but even there, I was coming apart.

He grinned then and went back to work.

And I, for the first time since my burning, lit my wayfarer lanterns and called to the lost. I was burnt, but so were my people. It was time, if not to heal, then to sit together bleeding.

He stayed with me, welcoming those who came in, so I didn't scare them with my piecemeal monstrosity of a body. Without a past to hold on to, he still found a way, and that way bound him forever to me. For even a library of the lost needed a librarian, and who better than one with no paths to return to.

To Immortalize Love

Safiya Bint Saleh

MᶜBRIDE'S FIRST VICTIM WAS a pretty young woman with a penchant for braiding flowers into her straw-colored hair.

Or so one could glean from her portrait. Unlike the majority of McBride's other subjects, her picture held a look of wonder on her face, one that could rival the red-lipped porcelain dolls decorating the windows of the toy shop in town. After all, she was the first to be trapped in a painting. She likely had no idea what fate awaited her when she followed McBride to his castle nestled in the woods.

Locals told a great many stories about her, but they said so much about all of McBride's victims. Given his penchant for targeting foreigners, it was likely that most of the locals spun their stories from whatever interpretation they made of the grotesque paintings hanging in his gallery.

There was, of course, one piece of truth that the entire town agreed upon: that on the eve of the new year, McBride mysteriously vanished.

Well, that had one very plausible theory: living amongst the tortured faces of his trapped victims must've driven him mad. No doubt he walked into one of his paintings himself, never to return.

Mona knew better.

McBride truly lived the life of a tortured artist. The trees in this part of the woods formed a canopy so thick that the castle lived under a constant shade of darkness. The artist clearly had no interest in combating this, as the castle was also draped in dull maroons and grays. Gothic indeed.

The only exceptions were the ornate gold frames decorating the entire length of the hallway.

"He had a way with landscapes," came a voice from behind, a staccato that echoed in the empty halls.

Mona glanced over her shoulder at the fair-haired baker's apprentice. If he considered a woman's bosom to be a landscape, she supposed his observation was correct. It was his luck that he had information on the victims his peers did not—she never would've chosen him otherwise.

Now, if one could look past the distraught expressions held by the subjects, the paintings were quite stunning. McBride had an incredible command of smoothly blending oil paints into scenes depicting sweeping cliffsides and rolling hills. There was a certain allure in the juxtaposition between his victims and the worlds he'd trapped them in. Take, for example, the woman with a silken saree, a royal no doubt, her strong brows forever drawn into a frown as she realized what McBride had done. One would expect to see her reclining on a divan at a Mughal palace, but she would live forevermore amongst highland cows chewing on cud.

The baker's apprentice seemed to take a liking to this piece too, casting a long glance at the victim's bronze skin, particularly her exposed waist under her blouse, which mirrored Mona's own coloring. "Don't touch it, Micah," she snapped, watching his fingers idly drift towards the textured canvas.

Micah froze, his eyes as wide as a spooked deer's. "I thought we were starting here."

Mona cast a glance at the works of art around them. McBride had arranged all thirty of them in falling order, from his first victim to the last. "We start with the one who can give us the most information," she said, dropping her hand into the pouch at her hip. The glass vials inside, precisely twelve of them, tinkled against each other.

"The one who last saw him," Micah said, leading them to a woman draped in furs. "The most fashionable woman to step foot in town."

Mona raised a brow. "Is that what drew McBride to her?"

Micah paused for a moment. "Perhaps. I will never be sure."

There was something about this painting, detailed and rich in a way the others were not. The subject was paler than the moon, dressed in barely more than slip save for the thick stole around her neck. She sat reclined in a chair on a balcony overlooking the sea, eyes closed, and face turned to the night sky like she was at peace with being trapped forever.

Perhaps she didn't know. Perhaps McBride was so charming that she never suspected him.

At a movement to her side, Mona clicked her tongue, watching Micah reach for the painting again. "You seem very interested in getting trapped inside."

A crease touched Micah's forehead as she handed him a vial. "I've touched them before. Nothing happened."

"That was before McBride disappeared, wasn't it?" she said. "Now drink."

She swirled the dark contents of her own bottle before tipping the potion to the back of her throat. As the bitter liquid burned against her insides, she tamped down the urge to retch.

Beside her, Micah paled beyond his already sallow complexion. That was easy. "Now?" he asked.

"Now." This time, she didn't protest as Micah reached for the painting. His fingers skimmed the textured surface, and then, like the tension breaking on still water, the canvas rippled, and his hand sank straight in.

Micah's eyes shot wide open. "I'm going in."

She gave a single nod. "I'm right behind you."

And with one solid leap, Micah disappeared into the painting.

A sour taste filled Mona's mouth as she ran her fingers along the gilded edges of the frame, but whether it was the potion or bile, she didn't know. She only knew that she had three attempts to get this right.

She rested her fingers against McBride's imagination of a balcony by the sea. It was warm, like water on the shores of a tropical island. Little waves formed at her disturbance, beckoning her in.

She rested a foot against the uneven bricks jutting from the wall.

And then she pushed right inside.

Mona had only been inside a painting once before.

In the farther parts of the world, McBride's crimes were folklore told by sailors docking for trade, often with a swashbuckling twist where the story would end with the sailors lopping the artist's head off. It had some of the young girls tittering and hiding their blushing faces behind their muslin sarees, but, like Mona, none of them took it to be truth.

That changed when she was invited to dine with the recently deceased zamindar's widow.

The woman, who could be no older than forty, smiled at Mona over her cup of chai. "You have a fire in you."

Mona, unsure of what to say, followed the woman silently to her parlor. The widow's father had married her to the zamindar, a man twice her age, when she was only fifteen. She gave the zamindar ten children in ten years, and he rewarded her by taking on a second wife, then a third, and then a fourth. When news of his death broke, she stood at his funeral with a solemn face but shed no tears.

In that parlor, taking up the majority of the west wall, was a grand painting. Mona had seen nothing like it, such a realistic depiction of the zamindar with his peppered brows raised in a quizzical expression.

At her side, his widow whispered, "He is real."

Mona briefly thought of running. But instead, she accepted the woman's open palm as she said, "Would you like to visit him with me?"

The sensation of passing through the canvas felt just as it did last time, like walking through a forest made of silk. She pushed forward with her hand, and the painting fell away, exposing the lingering rays of a waning crescent illuminating the veranda.

And sitting there, next to a glass table, was the lady in furs. The subject of the painting. McBride's final victim.

The woman brushed a curtain of ebony hair over her shoulder. "The young man went to observe the scenery," she said, swirling a flute of champagne.

Mona's eyes drifted to her surroundings. As with the painting, she made out the waves crashing against the cliff which the veranda hung over, and to the sides went down two sweeping staircases. But when she turned, all she faced was blankness. A wall of white, rough and textured, a piece of the picture McBride never could've accounted for when he painted the breathless scenery opposite it.

And to Mona's left, peering at the woman through the gaps between the balcony's balusters, was Micah.

"Do you consider yourself the scenery?" Mona asked the woman, keeping her eyes trained on Micah.

The woman bent down to look at the young man, exposing the deep neckline on her gown. She hummed to herself as Micah flushed red, then caught Mona's eye and skittered up the stairs.

The woman took a sip of her drink. "Men cannot be helped."

Mona kept her eyes on the young man, who promptly raced up to her heels, twiddling his thumbs like a schoolchild caught misbehaving by his teacher. "And if they grow to become the likes of McBride?"

The corners of the woman's lips lifted. "A world without monsters is heaven, my dear."

Mona opened her mouth to make a response, but Micah strolled over to the lady, holding his hand out to her. "We come to bring McBride to justice, my lady. We come to rescue you."

Mona bit back a laugh. "You are ambitious, Micah."

The lady in furs watched Mona's face before taking a sip of her champagne. Micah's hand remained outstretched. "This one would make an interesting monster."

Micah dropped his arm, licking his lips as he looked between the two women. "Mona, we don't have much time. We should find McBride."

Mona drew a vial from her pouch and tossed it to him. "I'm not certain he's here."

With a ginger touch, Micah held it out to the lady in the furs. "Ah, she will help us find him."

For a second time, the lady shunned his offering. "This place is my punishment as much as it is my paradise. I must stay here." She cast a long look at the horizon, at the never-ending expanse of sea.

"We will help you," Micah insisted, this time pushing the vial into the woman's hand.

The woman smiled, calmly placing the potion on the table. "Silly boy. Your companion never planned for me to leave."

As Mona wrapped her arm protectively around her pouch, Micah frowned. "Why would we not save a victim?"

The lady in furs turned her eye on Mona. "Because she came to find McBride, not me. And yet, to her dismay, he's not here."

The woman was ridiculing her, but what could Mona say? She deserved it. "It was wrong of me to assume so much. Perhaps you can point us in the right direction."

The lady in furs downed the rest of her champagne. "All I know is that I was always too much for him. He could never be with someone like me."

There were no right words to say, and even if there were, the moment was stolen by Micah, who shook his head. "No, this is not right. We cannot use her and then leave."

Mona leveled him with a stare. "I have a limited supply of potions. Our first priority is to find and subdue McBride. Why don't you give her your potion and stay behind yourself?"

At this, Micah's mouth hung open. His face flushed, but out of fear this time. He glanced at Mona, and then at the woman, and then, with a grand gesture at the ocean, said, "Sail away, my lady. You cannot subject yourself to this."

Mona knew the answer before the lady spoke. "There is nowhere to go. In the morning, I will wake, and I will be back here."

As Micah fiddled with the potion, Mona stepped back to the blank wall behind them, motioning for the young man to go first.

With a deep breath, he flung the potion into the back of his throat and dove straight into the canvas.

The wall rippled once under his weight, and then he was gone.

As Mona turned to leave, the woman's words echoed behind her. "My dear, I made McBride into the monster he is today. Be careful."

Mona pushed a hand through the wall, feeling the silkiness of the portal between her fingers. She glanced over her shoulder at the woman once more, taking in her languid posture, her complete indifference to being abandoned. "You will lose your mind here."

The woman sighed. "Perhaps this is my hell. What will yours be?"

Mona said nothing and disappeared into the wall.

In Mona's homeland, the dead were buried in white cloth. There were no viewings and no delays. The zamindar's case was no different—he passed during the night and was buried before the dawn prayer.

The zamindar's widow led her into a room that held the rich aroma of turmeric, cumin, and coriander roasting in mustard oil. "He loved to eat."

And this she said as she led them into a dining space that was eerily similar to the one hand-crafted out of teak wood in her own home.

But as Mona questioned everything, questioned the reality of the whole ordeal, the zamindar's widow gently guided her to the steaming thali tray waiting for them on the table. It was full of delicacies Mona never thought she would see in one meal. There was an assortment of bhortas, all different kinds of mashed vegetables and proteins in rich spices, accompanied by steaming rice and various fried goods. Sitting in a pot of its own, sizzling like it had been brought from the stove just a moment ago, was a meat curry.

This could not be. It was impossible. One could not walk into a painting like this.

But the zamindar's widow prompted her: "Eat."

And when Mona plucked a piece of meat from the pot and popped it into her mouth, hot, spicy, and fragrant, she knew that it must be real. It may be magic, it may be something so dark she may never return from it whole, but it was real.

The zamindar's widow watched her with a smile. "Do you like it?"

Mona could not speak, only nodding her head in awe.

And then, without warning, the widow grabbed the thali with her henna-stained hands and hurled it to the floor.

As Mona froze, the widow's smile returned, but her eyes glinted with a hint of vengeance. "Now watch."

Micah was not pleased, but he had yet to learn that his opinions mattered little to a woman like Mona.

It was to her benefit that Micah was quite the textbook. As the baker's apprentice, he heard much of the morning gossip while the townspeople collected their morning bread. And because of that, he knew who came into town, who went out of town, and who came, but never left.

When Mona held out a vial to him this time, he crossed his arms and frowned. "I will not help you if you do not rescue these women."

She continued holding it out. "Then you must have figured out where McBride is. Tell me."

He gulped so hard that the apple in his throat bobbed. "That is not a fair argument."

She snorted. "Then go home, Micah."

She knew he would not. He wanted to punish McBride—how could he take all these beautiful women Micah had seen and enforce such a fate upon them?

He downed the potion with only one complaint: "Does it have to taste so horrid?"

Mona, swallowing down bitterness herself, sighed. "Do you think magic so easy to acquire?" He said nothing, so she nodded at the paintings. "The middle one. The height of his crimes."

They walked up to a fair woman with rounded curves that had birthed many a babe. She wore an expression of shock with a hand over her mouth, clearly stifling a scream.

"It makes sense," Micah's voice was barely a whisper. "She has a softness to her, unlike the lady in furs."

They silently stepped into the painting.

McBride had left this woman, a poet, in a rolling plain filled with flowers of all colors.

The grass whispered songs through the breeze, and birds chirped somewhere.

But sitting on a picnic blanket, her back turned to Mona and Micah, the poet said nothing.

Micah set off first, dropping to his knees in front of the woman. He grabbed her shoulders and shook, and Mona knew before she saw the woman's face that she did not have the strength to fight.

Surrounding the woman was the story of her life. Ballads and sonnets written in her hand told of her yearning for McBride, her loneliness at being trapped, and her sorrow at losing everything she had loved.

But clutched in her first were words written by another. By *McBride*.

You have her eyes.

A chill crept down Mona's spine as she passed the paper to Micah. "There was another woman all along. He can't be here."

They turned to the poet. Her chest rose and fell in steady motion, but her stormy gray eyes were fixed at the never-ending horizon with a gaze as blank as her heart must have felt.

Micah's voice was weak as he turned to Mona. "You will leave a woman like her behind, too?"

Mona, who had not bothered to sit, turned to the canvas behind them. "We'll come back for her."

Micah stalked up to her, clenching his fists. "What if she dies?"

Mona sighed. "Keep her alive till I come back for her, then. Will you do that?"

And once again, Micah silently crumpled and followed her back to the castle.

The zamindar was a shadow of the person he used to be—frail and wrinkled where he once boasted a potbelly and enough strength to strangle a man with his bare hands.

Clutching a rag, he fell to his knees and mopped up the spilled food in silence.

And his widow—no, his *wife*—clicked her tongue in disappointment, because he did not wear a turban, he did not dress his best when there was a guest present.

The widow jeered at her husband and kicked the waste in his direction. "You mock me by serving old food."

Mona, trained in the art of politeness like all women of their culture, gasped. "It tasted delicious—"

But the widow stopped her with a firm glance. "No. Your father would let you serve this? Your uncles?"

Mona could not speak, for they both knew the truth. They could never.

"Men will not learn humility until they are taught," said the widow.

The man kept his frame small and silent as he exited the room.

"Must we stoop to their level?" Mona asked.

There was no hesitation in the widow's voice. "We must, until our mothers and our grandmothers, and the women who birthed them, are avenged."

Mona feared this knowledge, feared the power that came with it. "And what of men like the one who created this world for you?"

The widow sighed. "One man to destroy another. They will burn each other to the ground."

Mona found herself in front of the first victim.

There was a trajectory to be seen here. A lady resigned to her punishment. A woman broken by her imprisonment. And the one who started it all, with her straw-colored hair and cherry-red lips?

Micah shook his head as Mona encouraged another drink. "I must eat first. I cannot. It makes me ill."

Mona stared at his sallow face and gaunt cheeks. This adventure had clearly taken its toll on him, but did not magic always? It was a dark and dangerous thing, and it would take all that they had to give.

But she had to persist.

"We will have our answers soon," she promised, hoping it sounded encouraging.

Micah barely held it down this time, leaning against the wall with a hand against his mouth, his face somewhat green. "Perhaps we should eat some bread."

Mona ran her finger along the dusty details of the gold frame. "It will all come back up. One more painting, and we will be finished."

Micah was clearly more agitated than he was at the start, and she could not blame him. But this was the last one, and then they would have their answer. After all, there was only one other woman in this gallery with gray eyes.

And so, she asked him what he knew of the first victim, and with his face pale, he said, "She brought the light that illuminated the darkness where he lived."

And off they went to visit McBride's first victim.

One would think that the artist would not choose a bedroom as his setting. Maybe the brilliant chill of the mountains or the raging cliffs by the sea, but not a room in a tower of stone, draped in simple blacks and whites. And there, opposite to Mona and Micah, a bed made of stone, and on it, a woman lying in stillness, her hands folded gently over her chest.

Micah spoke the very words that Mona thought. "She is dead."

And it was clear what McBride had wanted all along. To preserve his memory—the memory of the woman he loved and lost.

And all the women after her, who made him feel something, he preserved forever, so that they would never leave him like the girl with the straw-colored hair.

Micah looked like he'd empty the contents of his stomach over the floor.

Mona ignored him, staring at the white flower buds braided into the young woman's hair. The air held still as she plucked one, holding it close to her own beating heart.

Snowdrops were seasonal flowers.

She held it out to Micah. "This was picked no more than a day ago. The original painting had red flowers."

"So, he's here." Micah's eyes were darting around the room now, but there were no doors in sight. The only way in and out was the canvas itself.

The words felt heavy on Mona's tongue. "He must have the ability to go in and out of the paintings. So, he must be out there."

Micah shook his head, muttering again and again, "No, no, it can't be."

He barely caught the potion she tossed him. "You'll back away when we've come this far? Why are you so afraid of him?"

She left without waiting for his response.

When Micah finally deigned to join her, he fell to his knees, groaning in pain. "I cannot confront McBride now," he said, taking deep breaths between his words.

"You can," said Mona, standing patiently in front of him.

Micah turned his head toward her. "How? He could be anywhere. We could be next."

Mona glanced at the end of the hallway, where a set of doors awaited them, slightly ajar. The sight sent her heart racing. There wasn't a single man trapped in this gallery. If anyone was at risk, it was her. "We can't give up," she said. "Not when we're so close."

"You think he's in his studio?" Micah's voice was a whisper, as if McBride could hear him.

"If he hasn't been seen in town, but he left flowers in the painting..." She didn't have to say more.

All Mona knew was that McBride was in the castle. And what better place to hide than his studio? No matter what Micah thought, she would see this through to the end. With a deep breath, Micah hauled himself upright. "It'll be over soon. We're doing this for justice."

Mona gave a solemn nod. "For justice."

As he set off, Mona at his heels, her pulse roared in her ears. This was it. The moment she had been waiting for.

Micah pushed the door open, exposing the lush carpets adorning every inch of the floor. Like the rest of the castle, it was still, silent, cold, and they walked through it like a sharpened knife slicing through sinew and bone.

"Be careful," Mona whispered. "He could be anywhere."

But Micah was brave now. He had already found his target, drawn to the one thing that stood out in the room: an easel set by the window, and on it, an unfinished painting.

The details revealed themselves as they drew closer. Rough strokes of blue and brown, a room of some sorts, empty and barren.

"He's in there?" Micah asked, sweeping a glance across the rest of the room.

Mona paused and pointed at a mark in the far corner, barely a dot. "That must be him. He's clearly not in here with us."

Micah frowned. "That is merely a stain on an unfinished painting."

She clicked her tongue. "Must you resist everything I say? Look closer, it is him."

Micah barely concealed a sound of dissatisfaction as he leaned forward, but it was enough. He held the temples of his head, muttering, "I must eat soon. This has taken a toll on me."

Mona tilted her head. The young man was heralded in town for his looks—he could be chiseled out of stone, for all that anybody knew.

He had carved himself into the perfect subject.

And, as he peered at the unfinished painting, trying to find a face in the black dot, trying to fight back the effects of the poison she'd fed him, trying to follow the instructions that had led him to his fate, Mona pushed, and in fell Micah to the painting.

He had no time to utter a cry, but the canvas captured his mouth wide open, blue eyes wide with shock as he realized what she had done.

He was a beautiful subject indeed.

It was a pity he had led McBride to all his victims.

He would pay the price.

With a sigh, Mona strolled to the fireplace, tugging at the bed sheet draped above it. As it fell away, she glanced up at the mantle. For, sitting there, drawn crudely into the corner of a painting of a world ablaze, was the artist himself, the hair singed off his head, his beard alight with embers.

"I still have the blacksmith and stable boy to handle," she said, as she stared at the parts of his screaming face that were not obscured by the orange flames. "This world needs to be a safe place before those women can return. There is a thrill in it, though—is that what you enjoyed? Did Micah enjoy handpicking your victims for you? Perhaps I should take the two of you home as my trophies."

There was silence, as neither man could answer.

She would silence them all one day.

After all, the pieces were set in place. The men would come to find her, and she would end them.

Let them burn each other to the ground. She would wait.

The God of the Leftmost Door

M.R. ROBINSON

F OR TWENTY-NINE YEARS, THE dead woman in the blood-smudged brown shawl sits alone in the back booth and doesn't say a word to anyone.

You watch her. For twenty-nine years, you watch the dead woman who won't so much as meet your eyes from across the room, and you don't say a word. You just watch.

After all, it isn't your job to talk to her. It's your job to stand by the front door. To welcome the newly dead to the last pub they'll ever visit—to take their coats and hats and mucky boots, maybe give their hands a reassuring squeeze if they have that white-eyed and terrified look, and point them towards the bar, where the god of good whiskey is almost always already filling another glass. Once the dead make it through the front door, your job is done. The others take over: the god of dark beer, or the god of pickled eggs and sausage rolls, or the god of long conversations after midnight by the fireside.

You're the god of the entryway. Not the god of staring at the woman in the back booth. Still, you can't help yourself. Most guests stick around for an hour or two. Others are in a hurry. Sometimes your guests need a few days before they're ready to walk through the other door: the leftmost door, the one that leads out of the in-between and to the other side. No one stays for a year. No one stays for twenty-nine years. No one but the dead woman with the blood-smudged brown shawl tugged tight around her shoulders.

For twenty-nine years, she's looked exactly the same. Stout and square-jawed and frowning, only ever frowning, at the table. Twenty-nine years, and she hasn't aged a day. You're no good at guessing mortal ages, but you can tell she's—not young, no, but too young to be dead. Younger than she'd planned, surely: no more than five or six decades through whatever life she'd imagined for herself when something happened to bloody her shawl and send her here.

You're not *scared* of her. You're not scared of anything. You're a god, and she's a dead woman. But—

"You ought to say something," the god of swept floors murmurs, their voice impossibly soft, unbearably sweet, and so close to your ear that your stomach knots up like a boot lace.

"You startled me," you snap, and take a clumsy step away from them. The words come out sharper than you'd intended. Nothing comes out right when you're talking to the god of swept floors. Still, when you twist to see that sideways smile and those spilled-oil eyes, your voice softens: "Anyhow, it's not my job to say something. My job is—"

"To open the door," the god of swept floors finishes. They rap their broom against the jamb for emphasis. "So, go on, then. Why don't you help her through *that* one too?"

You shift your attention to the leftmost door: nondescript, a little crooked on the hinges. There are gods for nearly everything, but in all your time in the in-between, there's never been a god of the leftmost door. It never seemed necessary: most dead folk have no trouble with the door, in the end, not even those who need time to calm down first. The dying is the hard part.

"She's been dead a long time," you say haltingly. Time's a funny thing for gods, even little ones like you, but you know enough to suspect that twenty-nine years is a long time for a mortal woman to sit in one place frowning at the table, dead or alive. "She must be scared."

"So, talk her out of being scared," the god of swept floors says, like it's simple. "She can't stay forever. If the big gods find out we have a squatter, we'll never hear the end of it."

"Why me?" you ask. Futile. Too late. The god of swept floors has already asked, and you're no good at saying no to the god of swept floors. Not when they're smiling again.

"Because you're the best of us," they say, which makes your cheeks warm and your chest tight, and point to the back with their broom. "And because no one else will do it."

So, you go. Fighting against the impulse to beg the god of swept floors to walk with you, you go, and for the first time in twenty-nine years, you aren't watching anymore. For the first time in more years than you can count, you're doing something more than loitering by the door.

"Ma'am," you begin.

The woman looks up, dark eyes under dark brows. Doesn't say a word. Looking at her head-on, you can finally see the raw, ruined wound above one eye where her skull has split: the thing that sent her here, the reason for her bloody shawl.

"Myra," she says. Somehow, she manages to make it sound like a threat.

You hold out your hands. "I know you're scared, Myra," you say as gently as you can. "But you don't need to be scared. I'm here to help. It's time for you to go."

"No. No, no. You don't know anything," she says, slow and low. Her mouth twists in a grimace so cold and strange and ugly that you take one step back and then another. "I'm not scared. I don't want your help. And I'll *tell* you when it's time for me to go."

You're not scared of her, because you're a god, because she's a dead woman, because you've never been scared of anything in all your life and you don't mean to start now. But—

You're not *not* scared of her, either.

If you had it your way, you'd spend another twenty-nine years sulking by the entryway. But things rarely seem to go your way, especially when the god of swept floors is involved.

"She's awful," you tell them. You're huddled together in the broom closet so the god of good whiskey won't catch you with a stolen bottle. Liquor doesn't do much for a god—doesn't even flush your cheeks. Your face feels hot anyway. It's the ritual of passing a bottle back and forth. The thrill of being here when you should be working. The way your skin buzzes when the god of swept floors laughs and thoughtlessly touches your wrist.

"She's just a prickly old woman. A mortal woman. Be brave!"

You're the god of the entryway; nothing in your job description says you ought to be brave when a dead woman with her head split halfway open gives you a look like she means to split yours, too. "She's scared," you say, more to yourself than to the god of swept floors. "Scared and lashing out."

That's all it is, isn't it? *She's* the scared one. Not you. So, when you're finally done hiding in the broom closet—when you're done letting the god of swept floors talk you into foolishness or courage or both—you gather every last scrap of strength you've got and try once more to get her through the leftmost door.

"One drink," you suggest, "and then it's time to go."

"No," she says, and bares her crooked teeth at you like a dog. "No."

You try again the next night, and the night after that too. You describe everything waiting on the other side as best you can. Not the details, but the important parts: the stillness, the softness, the way she'll never have to be afraid again.

"No," she says. "No. I don't want to go."

No, she says, *no, no,* so often you begin to begin to find her more exasperating than intimidating. One night, she accepts a frothing mug instead of waving you away. She takes one sip, then pulls a face like you've served her piss instead of stout.

"No," she says.

At last your fraying patience triumphs over your nerves. Doing your best to channel the easy confidence of the god of swept floors, you sit across from her. "You're afraid of death. That's nothing to be ashamed of. But you can't stay here, Myra. I'm sorry, but you can't."

"I'm not afraid of death."

"Look," you say, more wheedling now, and gesture at a pale-haired man at the bar with a hole blown through his middle and a friendly smile.

He's only been dead for a few hours, but with the help of the god of good whiskey, he's taken to it well enough. "Why don't you see if this fellow will walk with you? That way you won't have to go through the door alone."

"Stop it," she snaps—snarls, almost, more animal than dead woman—and slams her hands down on the table between you.

You stop.

"I'm waiting for someone." There's a wild look in her eyes; her hands are shaking so badly that you'd reach for her, more instinct than common sense, if you thought she'd let you. "I'm not going through the door with a stranger. I'm not going through the door without her."

"Oh," you breathe, understanding settling like a stone on your chest. You can't seem to find any other words. "Oh, Myra. I'm sorry. I—"

"I'm not going anywhere without my Annie," Myra says again. She touches two fingers to one brow, just below the edges of the wound that sent her to you. "One time I did, and look where it got me."

Your stomach aches like you might be sick. You want to lie. You want to say something comforting. Offering comfort—guiding people through the entryway—that's always been your job. You've never had to do the hard part. You've never had to tell the truth.

But when you reach for some gentle falsehood, you can't find the words. You can only picture the god of swept floors with the cosmos in their eyes and a broom in their hands and *Be brave!* on their lips.

"We don't get everyone here," you say. "Only people like you or like him, who might need a bit of extra help. If she's alive, she'll go somewhere else in the in-between. Not here. If she isn't, she might already be on the other side."

She stares at you for a moment, for a lifetime. She licks her lips; her throat moves. When she finally manages to speak, the words come out sharp and choked at once. "I see. Would it be hard, then, to find her on the other side?"

"It would be hard," you say. "Not impossible. But it's not quite like this, on the other side. The shapes of things aren't so familiar there. People aren't so familiar."

"And if she's somewhere else in-between?"

"I'm sorry. We aren't allowed to help with that. If we helped one person, we'd have to help everyone, and—"

"You aren't allowed," Myra begins, her voice rising, then stops herself. Her gaze drops to her trembling hands. After a minute, she looks up, dark eyes wet and red at the edges. "One drink, you said. One last drink. Does the offer still stand?"

"One drink," you say. "And then it's time to go."

You place one hand on hers. She doesn't pull away. This time, she doesn't say no.

"We really shouldn't be here," you hiss. This corner of the cellar is the god of good whiskey's domain, and breaking the rules always makes your chest hurt. But the god of swept floors only laughs as they pluck a dusty bottle from the shelf. With one hand, they hoist their prize; with the other, they squeeze your arm.

"You aren't afraid, are you?" they ask.

You don't know how to answer, so you don't. Instead you tuck your hands under your arms like you've caught a chill—though every inch of you feels warm—and follow them up the stairs, across the room, and all the way to the back booth.

When the god of swept floors fills three glasses, Myra smiles. A thin, watery-eyed smile, but a smile—the first you've seen from her. She lifts the glass and sends a few amber drops across the table. "To good health and a long life, I would have said, once upon a time."

"To peace," you offer. "To rest."

"To the leftmost door," the god of swept floors says, and clinks their glass against yours. The two of you are pressed terribly close together in the booth—your knees knocking, your thighs bumping. And they keep *looking* at you, smiling like they're proud. Like you've done something good. Like you've done something more than break a dead woman's heart.

You can't look at them. You drink deeply, for all the good it will do, and add another splash to your glass.

"You were right, you know," Myra says. She tilts her glass to one side and then the other, whiskey aglow in the candlelight. "Right and wrong, both. I wasn't afraid until tonight."

"It's a fine thing to be afraid of death," you say.

"I'm afraid of being alone," she says without meeting your gaze. "Not death. But being alone—well. I've never been alone, not ever. I always had my Annie, didn't I? Always, always, I had my Annie."

"Tell us about her," the god of swept floors says in that way they have: like it's a challenge. Like they aren't afraid of anything.

At first you don't think Myra means to answer. After a moment's silence, she downs her glass and meets your gaze. "We were only girls when we met. She was everything I wasn't. Tall and blue-eyed—like the sea, I mean, not the sky—and beautiful. Wickedly smart. And fearless. Fearless, more than anything. I was so scared of everything. Scared even to touch her hand where someone might see. She was never scared."

Your mouth feels strangely dry. "You were—?"

"She called me her wife," she says, knuckles gone white around the glass in her hands. "We weren't. We couldn't. Not truly."

"True enough," the god of swept floors murmurs.

"What else?" you say. You're hardly thinking. Not about the rules, not about the things you ought and ought not to do. Not about anything other than Myra, who is here, and Annie, who is not. "What did she do? Where do you think she would be now?"

"Enough," Myra says, clipped and quavering in equal measure. She dabs at her eyes with the hem of her shawl. "Oh, enough, enough. She'd be an old woman, if she's living. An old woman long done with her grieving, surely. What of you? Do gods fall in love?"

"Some do," you say, thinking of the lovers you've known in your day: the god of clean dishes and the god of broken glasses, always squabbling fondly in the kitchen, or the way the god of long conversations by the fireside after midnight looks with such soft eyes at the god of companionable silences. "Others don't."

"And what do you know about love?" she asks.

You don't know anything about love. You know that sometimes you feel a twisting in your middle when the god of swept floors leans on their broom and waggles their eyebrows at you. You know that sometimes, sometimes, your mouth goes dry and your palms go damp when they prop their broom against the bar and touch your shoulder. When they flash that rakish sideways smile—

You know that you can feel their eyes on you as you fumble for an answer.

You fold your hands in your lap. "Not enough."

"Well, don't let my tears talk you out of it." She smiles again—still wan, but enough to make her shining eyes crinkle at the corners. "It's a scary thing, love. An awful, ugly thing. A beautiful thing and a brave thing. Oh, I spent so long hoping I'd find her again. Hoping she'd find me. But it was enough to be together for a little while. It has to be enough, doesn't it?"

"I wish we could help," you say. "We would if—"

Myra exhales, bone-brittle, and wipes once more at the corners of her eyes. "If you were allowed. I know. Is this it, then? Am I out of time?"

Yes, you ought to say. *Yes, yes, it's time for you to go.*

"Tomorrow," you say.

The god of swept floors touches your knee questioningly beneath the table, which makes you flinch so hard the glasses rattle. You seize their wrist. "We'll be back," you say. And before Myra can reply, you've dragged the god of swept floors all the way to the broom closet.

"What—?"

"Annie," you whisper. "We have to look for her."

The god of swept floors looks baffled, doubtful, delighted, and then all three at once. "What if she's alive?"

"Then everything's the same. But if she *is* dead—if she's waiting in the wrong place—" You falter, hardly knowing what's come over you, then charge ahead: "I'm not the kind of god who drags terrified people through a door because the rules say so. I'm the kind of god who takes their hats and holds their hands and helps them enter on their terms, when they're ready. I may only be the god of the entryway, but I mean to act like it. I mean to *try.*"

"Look at you," the god of swept floors breathes. They touch your chin, tentative, then take your face in both hands. "Oh, look at you! You're not only anything. If you think it's worth trying—tell me what to do. Tell me what to do, and I'll do it."

Your heart catches and jumps like kindling in a fire at the heat of their touch. And you know. At once, you know what it means to be a different kind of god. To be the god of the entryway is to be a god who waits, never the first to act. But to be the god of the leftmost door—

"Go, go," you say. "Check every house in the in-between. I'll keep her here. We ought to try, don't you think?"

"We ought to try," they echo, the strangest look in their eyes. They release you. And then they're gone.

When the door opens, you're kneeling behind the bar with a scrap of paper in your hands, reviewing the third draft of a note to the god of swept floors. At the sound of the creaking entryway door, though—in desperate need of the attention of the god of well-oiled hinges—you stand up so quickly that you knock your head on the lip of the bar.

Your vision swims. It takes a moment for the scene to come into focus. The god of swept floors stands silhouetted in the entryway, their broom in one hand, another figure at their side. "Sorry," you say to no one in particular, grabbing at your aching head. "I'm sorry, I—*oh.*"

"We have company," the god of swept floors says.

"Where can a woman get a drink around here?" the stranger asks.

It's an old woman's voice, worn but warm. You recognize the music of her accent. And—you recognize *her.* She's different than in Myra's telling. Older, certainly, with her hair short-cropped and silver, one wrinkled hand holding a cane. But she's the same, too: tall and blue-eyed and wearing a smile nothing short of fearless.

"Annie, oh, Annie, we've been waiting," you manage, tripping over your words as you round the bar, "here, here, right this way—"

She doesn't answer. She doesn't so much as look at you. She's already dropped her coat; she's already moving across the room. And before you've so much as picked her coat up off the sticky, well-swept floor, she's in Myra's arms.

You clutch her coat to your chest. You don't want to intrude. But you've been staring for twenty-nine years, and you can't bring yourself to stop just because there are two women in the corner instead of one, two women who fit together like they'd never spent a single moment apart. Annie draws Myra close, kisses her, then pulls back like it's enough just to look.

You turn away, blinking wetly, and find the god of swept floors at your side like they've been there all along.

"Dead for a fortnight," they say. "No one down the road could get her through the door."

"You found her," you say, then laugh at the raggedness of your own voice. You're exhausted, giddy, dazed. "I can't believe you found her."

"Only because you told me to look."

"Only because you told me to try."

There's a thousand things you want to say. A thousand and a thousand more. But you feel like you've forgotten every word you've ever known. You feel like you've forgotten everything but the shine of their eyes and the crook of their smile.

"You dropped something, by the way," the god of swept floors says. They press a scrap of paper into your palm, fingers lingering a moment too long against your wrist. "Swept it up while you were staring at those two. Or at least I think it's yours. Take a look."

"No," you croak. It was a draft, only a draft—

When you unfold the note with shaking hands, you see that it's not a draft at all. You see that it's exactly right.

Below the place where you have written *I do not know enough about love, but I would like to learn more,* the god of swept floors has written *I think we ought to try.*

"This way," Myra is saying to the woman at her side, "this way, the door on the left—nothing to be scared of, my love, my darling girl, nothing at all—"

You cram the paper into your pocket. You do not look at the god of swept floors.

You take their hand in yours.

The leftmost door opens, light like an ocean gleaming on the other side. Myra looks over her shoulder, catches your eye, and smiles. She reaches for Annie's hand, too.

Together, the two women cross the threshold. Together, they are there. Together, they are gone. And for the first time in all your long years, you understand what it means to be scared; for the first time, you understand what it means to be brave.

Exit

M. STEVENSON

YOU'VE WANDERED THROUGH PLACES unsettling and fantastical, witnessed wonders and horrors and impossibilities. Now you emerge into a familiar place. The last time you stood here, this forest of doors was draped in sheets of winter, and your steps left shadowed prints like a trail of ink across a white page. Now, chartreuse stipples the dark branches; the gold of crocuses shines between tree roots.

You pause to drink it in: the richness of damp earth; the breeze that stirs your hair, promising warmth and growth; the doors, countless, endless, each a possibility.

One calls to you, and you reach for the handle. It opens to your touch, as if it's been waiting for you this whole time.

You step across the threshold.

You leave the door open, for the ones who come behind.

About The Authors

ABOUT THE AUTHORS

EDITOR BIOGRAPHIES

M. Stevenson is the author of *Behooved* and other novels for adults and teens. Her poetry and prose have appeared in publications including *Small Wonders, PodCastle, Barely South, The Florida Review,* and *Poets Reading the News.* An avid swing dancer and amateur naturalist, she's often found dancing Lindy Hop or wandering the woods talking to birds and plants. She is based in the Finger Lakes region of New York.

C.J. Subko is a dreamer and a dabbler. She has a Ph.D. in Clinical Psychology, which makes her highly qualified to think too much. Her short fiction publications include *Inner Worlds* (May 2025), *Small Wonders* (November 2024), *Morgana le Fay* (Flame Tree Press; March 2025), *Red Line* (From Beyond Press; August 2025), and *The Deadlands*

(April 2025). She is a member of the HWA, SFWA, and Codex. She can be found at www.cjsubko.com and next to the Lake on sunny days.

CONTRIBUTOR BIOGRAPHIES

Claire Jia-Wen is a speculative fiction writer originally from the 626 and has been published in *khōréō* and *Clarkesworld*. A Viable Paradise and Clarion alum, she is currently getting her PhD in human-computer interaction.

Sara S. Messenger is a disabled East and West Asian writer from the US. She won the 2024 Nebula Award for Best Game Writing with her team. Her work has appeared in *Nightmare Magazine; Strange Horizons; The Year's Best Fantasy, Volume 2*; and more. You can find more and forthcoming work at sarasmessenger.com.

B.L. Jasper lives in New Hampshire and writes books for teens and adults. More of her short fiction can be found in *A Coup of Owls* literary magazine. When she is not writing, you can find her doing puzzles, journaling in her hobonichi, or taking her kids on a bit of adventure. Learn more at bljasper.com.

Michael Bettendorf (he/him) is a multi-genre writer from the Midwest. His short fiction has appeared at *Cosmic Horror Monthly, Mythaxis Magazine, the Drabblecast,* and elsewhere. His debut experimental horror novel/gamebook TRVE CVLT was released by Tenebrous Press (Sept. 2024). His tech-noir/cyberpunk collection MIDWESTERN CHROME is forthcoming at Tenebrous Press (2026).

Michael works in a high school library in Lincoln, NE. Find him on Bluesky @BeardedBetts and www.michaelbettendorfwrites.com.

Ahmad Addam holds a Master's degree in Public Health with a specialization in Creative Writing. Alongside his studies, he worked as a Research-MEAL for a peacebuilding and conflict sensitivity organization based in Lebanon. Since 2021, he has co-run QuillerSWANA and SWANApit, co-sister initiatives that provide platforms for Southwest Asian and North African writers to attend workshops, apply for mentorships, and participate in pitch contests aimed at restoring and amplifying SWANA voices. His poetry includes A Reaper in Beirut and Of South & Olive Oils, both published by *OvertlyLit*. He is also contracted as a poet for *Honeytrap*, a novel by Kiana Krystle under PeachTree Teen, set for release in 2027.

MJ Huntsgood is a speculative thriller and horror author who enjoys exploring the use of perspective and deep POV in her work to find the nightmare not just in a situation, but within ourselves. She hopes you, like her, dream of leaving this boring dystopia where we work to earn the right to work, scroll past children starving on our personal wiretaps, and pick and choose if human rights are even remotely up for debate. She lives in Washington DC with her ever dwindling number of underwatered plants, 2 cats and trophy husband.

Brooke Lanier is the chaotic queer character at any Dungeons and Dragons table. What began as a simple love for stories snowballed into an MFA in Creative Writing from Western Colorado University. When Brooke's not writing fantasies or daylighting as an electrical engineer, she's probably watching eldritch horrors in the Feywild (AKA looking for moose in the Rocky Mountains).

Harper Kinsley is an asexual, disabled author and educator from the Midwest States. She is an advocate for mental health, especially in the area of obsessive compulsive disorder, and writes stories to uplift others and help them feel seen. Harper's work can also be found in a number of anthologies. and her debut novel, SPIKES, DICE & OTHER VARIABLES releases in fall of 2026.

Justin Carlos Alcala (he/him) is an award-winning Mexican-American novelist & short story writer. His works are most notable for their appearance in *Publisher's Weekly, the SLF Foundation Awards*, and the University of British Columbia project archives. Justin is a folklore fanatic, a history nerd, a tabletop gamer, and a time traveler. Alcala's fifty-plus short stories, novellas, and novels can be found in anthologies, magazines, journals, podcasts, and commercial publications. He currently resides with his dark queen, Mallory, their fey daughter, Lily, changeling son, Ronan, goblin-toddler, Asher, and hounds of Ragnarök, Fenrir and Hilda, in Bigfoot's domain. Where his mind might be is anyone's guess.

Fendy S. Tulodo is from Malang, Indonesia. He works with words and sound, trying to catch how time stretches or shrinks for different people, how bonds stay present even when they're long gone. By day, he sells motorcycles. At night, he becomes Nep Kid. He makes quiet, moody music and writes stories in whatever form feels right. His art sits in the space between what's said and what's actually felt.

Rukman Ragas is made up of earnest contradictions and temporary obsessions. A Tamil writer of speculative fiction from Sri Lanka, they are fascinated by tender horrors, hysterical resistance, and the thin lines between disgust and desire. Rukman is a grateful alumna of the Clarion West 2025 workshop through the Octavia E Butler Memorial scholarship and their short fiction has appeared in venues including *khōréō*, *Apex*, and *The Baltimore Review*. They are currently a fiction editor at *Otherside Spec*, a magazine of queer fantastic. When not wrangling his novel into shape, he can be found consuming an unhealthy amount of historical media or playing DnD.

Safiya Bint Saleh is an IT Analyst by profession who really considers herself to be a certified cat enthusiast. When she's not cuddling one of her furry friends, she is writing Fantasy stories about headstrong women who challenge the bounds of society inspired by her experience as a first-generation Bangladeshi-American woman. Raised in the Mid-Atlantic United States, Safiya currently lives with her spouse wherever the wind takes them, as long as there are cats involved.

M.R. Robinson is a scholar and teacher of Renaissance literature... but when she isn't talking about sonnets, she's probably writing or reading speculative fiction. A graduate of Clarion West and Viable Paradise, her work has appeared in publications including *Beneath Ceaseless Skies, Flash Fiction Online, We're Here: The Best Queer Speculative Fiction 2024*, and elsewhere. She is one of the co-founders of OTHERSIDE, a magazine of speculative fiction by 2SLGBTQIA+ authors. You can find her across social media @mruthrobinson or at www.m-r-robinson.com.

Content Warnings

CONTENT WARNINGS

The Flutist and the Glassblower in the Market of Souls: blood, suicidal ideation, abuse

The Seam Ripper Above God's Navel: child abuse, unhealthy relationships, body dysphoria, transphobia, religion, colonialism, death/murder, bodily harm, pregnancy/afterbirth, kidnapping, ableism

Good Girls of the Salt: domestic abuse, misogyny, starvation.

Somewhere in the Nowhere: none

Of Cedar and Sea: misogyny

The Unbroken Circle: violence, implied child death

The Eagles are Nesting at Pheasant Run: none

Roots: obsessive thoughts surrounding harming others, knives, and contamination, on page panic attack, child in distress

Thirteen Winters: graphic violence, murder, and witchcraft

The Door in Her Throat: family conflict, parental abuse (verbal), emotional distress, imagery of self-harm

The Library of the Lost: mentions of war

To Immortalize Love: misogyny, emotional and verbal abuse, death, violence, kidnapping

The God of the Leftmost Door: death, mention of violent death